"Why can't you leave me alone?"

Jassy cried desperately, her mind seeming to split in two. "I hate you!"

She wanted to believe that was true, but the truth was she no longer knew what she felt.

"Do you?" Leigh inquired, unmoved. "Or do you just hate me for saying what you don't want to hear?"

Those tiger's eyes seemed to burn into Jassy's gray ones, challenging and mesmerizing all at once so that Jassy was unable to drag her gaze away.

"Why don't you face up to the truth," he continued. "I don't mind admitting I want to make love to you. You're a very lovely girl. But it's more than that—you're something special. I knew from the first moment I saw you that I wanted you. I still do."

Kate Walker chose the Brontë sisters, the development of their writing from childhood to maturity, as the topic for her master's thesis. It is little wonder, then, that she should go on to write romance fiction. She lives in the United Kingdom with her husband and son, and when she isn't writing, she tries to keep up with her hobbies of embroidery, knitting, antiques and, of course, reading.

THE GOLDEN THIEF

Kate Walker

Harlequin Books

TORONTO • NEW YORK • LONDON
AMSTERDAM • PARIS • SYDNEY • HAMBURG
STOCKHOLM • ATHENS • TOKYO • MILAN

Original hardcover edition published in 1990
by Mills & Boon Limited

ISBN 0-373-15403-8

Harlequin Romance EasyRead edition February 1991

THE GOLDEN THIEF

For Noelle

CHAPTER ONE

'I WON'T do it!'

Jassy's tone was adamant, her wide grey eyes stony with rejection of the suggestion that had just been put to her.

'No, Sarah,' she continued emphatically. 'You can say what you like, but I will *not* work for that man.'

'Jassy, you can't mean it!' Her flatmate's tone was sharp with disbelief. 'You can't be thinking of turning this down.'

'I'm not thinking—I'm doing it. I'd have to be totally desperate even to consider it.'

'But a job like this comes up once in a blue moon. And correct me if I'm wrong, but I got the impression that you *were* desperate.'

And that was something she couldn't deny, Jassy admitted privately, pushing a disturbed hand through her long ash-blonde hair before picking up the knife she had dropped when her flatmate had made her announcement, and turning her attention to slicing tomatoes for the salad she was preparing for their evening meal, the unnecessary force of her actions revealing her inner turmoil only too clearly.

She *was* desperate, that was the problem. Her formerly thriving career as an actress had come to an abrupt halt when the play she had been appearing in had turned out to be a complete flop, closing after only three weeks, and for the past two months she had been what was euphemistically known as 'resting'—in other words, unemployed—and the situation showed no sign of righting itself.

She had been to several auditions, but had been unsuccessful, the parts going to other, more experienced actresses, and nothing else seemed to be forthcoming. As a result, she was stony-broke and bored out of her head, which was why she had turned to Sarah's older sister for help. Francesca Templeton ran a secretarial agency, and as Jassy had taken a shorthand and typing course at her parents' insistence she had hoped that the older woman would be able to find a temporary job to tide her over this difficult patch. She would take any job, she had said, but she hadn't anticipated *this* one.

A frown crossed Jassy's forehead as she thought back over the evening from the moment the phone had rung and Sarah had gone to answer it. She had come back into the kitchen with a smugly triumphant grin on her face.

'I told you Cheska would sort things out!' she declared brightly, helping herself to a stick of raw carrot and crunching it between firm white teeth.

'She's found me a job?' Jassy asked, and Sarah nodded, her eyes gleaming.

'And what a job! You've struck lucky this time, mate!'

'What is it? Sarah!' Jassy exclaimed protestingly as her friend smiled mysteriously. 'Tell me!'

'Leigh Benedict!' Sarah announced, rolling her eyes dramatically, then she broke into a wide grin at the look of bewilderment on Jassy's face.

'Leigh Benedict?' she echoed blankly. 'What——?'

'Oh, come on, Jassy! You're the actress——'

'I know of *the* Leigh Benedict, of course!' Jassy declared in exasperation. 'You don't have to be an actress to know about him—but you can't mean——'

'Oh, but I do,' Sarah put in firmly, her response leaving her friend at a loss for words. For a moment Jassy simply stared, her thoughts whirling.

'*The* Leigh Benedict,' she repeated at last, her voice shaking slightly as memories she had thought buried rushed into her mind.

'The Golden Thief himself. You lucky thing! What I wouldn't give for a chance to meet him—and you walk straight into a job as his secretary.'

'I haven't got it yet!' Jassy protested automatically, admitting to herself that, even if she was offered the job, she was unlikely to want to take it. 'What does he want a secretary for anyway?' she added, curiosity getting the better of her.

'To sort out his fan mail,' Sarah told her with a laugh. 'No—honest—it's true. His current secretary's in hospital—appendicitis—and he needs someone to deal with all the letters and generally keep things in order until she gets back. Of course, there'll be other work too. From what Cheska said he's pretty busy with negotiations for this new film he plans to direct, but the fan mail will be more interesting, don't you think? All those love-letters from adoring women, telling him their most secret fantasies.'

'What an awful thought!'

Jassy's face twisted into a grimace of distaste at the idea, and at the thought of the Leigh Benedict hysteria that seemed to have afflicted almost all the female population of Great Britain and America for the past five years. She distrusted such adulation instinctively, mainly because it concentrated on the actor's looks and lifestyle, rather than any critical appreciation of his work. Leigh Benedict was devastatingly handsome, there was no denying that. The blond good looks that had, in part, earned him the nickname of the Golden Thief in the popular Press would always make him stand out in a crowd, even in the film world, and, having seen him in person, Jassy knew that his physical attraction had in no way been exaggerated. But looks weren't everything and she had her own private reasons for believing that Leigh Benedict was not the sort of man she would like in the least. However tempting the idea of gaining inside knowledge of his projected film might be, the thought of working for him was positively distasteful.

Benedict's nickname of the Golden Thief had been acquired early on in his career when he had starred in a film with Anna Golden, a beautiful and well-established actress some years older than himself, who was married, for the second time, to another actor, David Carrington. Even while filming was still going on, rumours of a romance were rife, and a few months later Carrington had sued for divorce on the grounds of his wife's adultery with Leigh Benedict.

Jassy remembered those events vividly because they had occurred at a time when, knowing that acting was the only thing she wanted to do, she had devoured absolutely anything she could find on the subject in books, magazines and newspapers. Having seen Leigh Benedict in several television plays and his first film, she had been stunned by the power of his acting, and so had been delighted when he had won his first Oscar for the film in which he had appeared with Anna Golden.

The next morning the newspapers had been full of photographs of him, his blond hair gleaming in the spotlight, the gold statuette in one hand, and the actress clinging possessively to his other arm. One of the more popular papers, playing on the fact that David Carrington had also been strongly tipped for that year's Best Actor award, had added the caption, 'The Man Who Stole the Limelight—and Anna Golden', but in a later edition, with a fanciful play on words, that had been changed to 'The Golden Thief', and the name had stuck, in spite of the fact that the affair between Leigh Benedict and Anna Golden had never come to the marriage everyone had anticipated.

But it was not of Anna Golden that Jassy was thinking when she frowned uneasily and turned to Sarah again.

'Couldn't Cheska find something else?' she said slowly, her heart sinking as her flatmate shook her head firmly.

'It's this or nothing. There's very little on the books, and she has her regular girls to consider. She said you should count yourself lucky she was even offering it to you. She's only doing it because your background knowledge of the acting world gives you that extra edge on anyone else. They'd kill her if they knew she'd given you first chance of such a job.'

They were welcome to the job, Jassy reflected, admitting to herself that anyone else would probably jump at the chance of working for the man who had been described as the sex symbol of the century. But then anyone else would be able to face Leigh Benedict quite easily, and not always be remembering...

Almost three years before, when she had been nearing the end of her course at drama school, Jassy had been totally involved in a production of *Romeo and Juliet* which the final year students had been working on under the guidance of their tutor, Benjamin Carstairs, affectionately known as Benjy. Jassy, who, to her delight, had been given the role of Juliet, had thrown herself into the part with an intensity and commitment that had been given an added impetus when the news broke that a guest at one performance was to be Leigh Benedict himself. She had seen all the actor's films and some of his stage performances since she had come to London, and had always admired his brilliant acting even if she'd shied away from the mass adulation his fame brought him.

All the stories of his wealth, his jet-set lifestyle, the string of beautiful women whose names had been linked with his could in no way detract from the fact that Leigh Benedict was currently number one on any critic's list for best actor of the year—and deservedly so. He had a reputation for being savagely critical, and Jassy had felt that if she could win one word of praise, however small, for her performance, then she would know she really could act, and the fight she had had to get to drama school in the face of her parents' opposition would all have been worthwhile. To have the approval of such a master of his craft as Leigh Benedict would be like a dream come true.

On the day of the performance she had been sick with nerves, her hands fumbling with the heavy dark wig she was to wear, as she dressed and made up in the crowded dressing-room. But she knew that once she got on stage those nerves would vanish as they always did. She felt like this before every performance, only coming alive under the heat of the stage lights when she became the other person, the part she was to play, but tonight she felt so much worse because she desperately wanted everything to go right. She was keyed-up to give the performance of her life before Leigh Benedict, so much so that it hit her like a slap in the face when one of her friends who had taken a surreptitious peep through the curtains came back into the dressing-room looking decidedly glum.

'Don't get your hopes up, girls,' Louisa announced in response to a buzz of excited questions. 'It looks as if the great man isn't coming. Anna Golden's there, sitting in state beside Benjy as if she were the superstar and not the old has-been that she is, but I'm afraid lover-boy's not with her.'

'He's not coming?' Jassy exclaimed, and Louisa shot her a sympathetic glance.

''Fraid not. I suppose he thinks we lesser mortals aren't worthy of his attention now he's got his second Oscar. It's rotten luck for you though. This was going to be your big night, wasn't it? Your chance to catch the Golden Thief's eye and maybe win a name for yourself.'

'I wanted to know what he thought of me as an actress,' Jassy responded fervently, and heard Louisa's amused laughter.

'You're always so intense about things, Jassy! We all want to act, but success is the name of the game in this business—and Leigh Benedict is success personified. He's not just a star, he's the sun and the moon and the planets all rolled into one. No director's going to argue with him if he wants a particular co-star in one of his films, so he can make or break beginners like us with one word from that sexy mouth of his. Get him hooked, and there's no looking back.'

'I'm here to play Juliet, not get myself a lover.'

Jassy's laugh was a little uneven. She wasn't alone in her hostility towards the casting-couch phenomenon, her strong objections to the idea of success gained by knowing someone with influence, but, perhaps because she had had to fight so hard to get where she was, because she was determined to convince her parents that her desire to act was a serious conviction, her chosen career one she was determined to work at with all the dedication and ability of which she was capable, she had found that she took the matter much more seriously than many of her fellow students.

'I want to impress the actor, not the man.'

'Why stint yourself, kiddo, when you can do both? And looking like that you would have had a fair chance of doing just that.'

Louisa's gesture took in the long, dark blue velvet dress whose flowing lines made the most of Jassy's tall, slender figure, the low-cut, tightly laced bodice enhancing the soft curves of her breasts, giving her a cleavage for the first time in her life. The black wig added a touch of drama to the widely spaced soft grey eyes which Jassy sometimes felt were a little insipid when teamed with her own ash-blonde hair and naturally pale complexion. Heavy stage make-up had darkened her long, thick lashes, emphasising her fine cheekbones, and making her mouth look even fuller and softer so that she hardly recognised herself.

At that moment, a voice in the corridor outside warned them that the performance was about to begin. Louisa held up her hand, fingers firmly crossed.

'Knock 'em dead, kid! Who knows, perhaps your luck's in and the Golden Thief's turned up after all?'

But the first thing Jassy noticed when she went on stage was the empty seat in the front row, next to Benjy. It remained empty during the performance, but, after that first moment of bitter disappointment, she was too caught up in the world of the play to notice. But when the final words had been spoken and Jassy and the rest of the cast were taking their bows, that empty space struck her once more as silent evidence of Leigh Benedict's arrogant lack of interest in their efforts, and she felt a strong surge of anger rush through her.

Only when the costumes had been put away and almost everyone had gone home did the actor put in an appearance. Jassy was the only one of the students to see him arrive, and that was only because she was waiting for Sarah and her current boyfriend who had promised her a lift home and who were, as always, very late.

She didn't particularly mind waiting, feeling the need to be alone while she was still in the throes of the let-down she always experienced after a performance, something which was especially difficult to cope with on this particular occasion, and so, because of her mood, she shrank back into the shadow of a wall as a sleek, powerful car drew up outside the main entrance to the college.

From her hiding-place she watched unobserved as Leigh Benedict sauntered up the steps as if he owned the place, meeting Benjy and Anna Golden at the door. His skin glowed from the early summer sun, his bright hair was bleached almost white at the front, and his strong body was very casually dressed in well-worn denim jeans and a black T-shirt with a light cotton jacket slung carelessly over one shoulder, the casual clothes seeming to imply that he had been doing nothing very important that night, but had simply not bothered to turn up. Jassy watched, her resentment growing by the minute, as he took Anna Golden's hand, pressing a kiss against the back of her fingers with elaborate courtesy, and murmured an easy greeting to Benjy, his words drifting easily to where she stood, biting her lip in frustration and anger.

'So how was your day on the beach?' Anna asked, the faint tartness of her tone belied by the way she slid her hand under Leigh's arm and pressed herself close up against him. Jassy heard the actor's contented sigh.

'It was idyllic. Sun, sand and sea, what more could you ask? I suppose I missed the production of the year?' he added, addressing his remark to Benjy without a hint of embarrassment or apology.

'I thought it went very well,' Benjy responded affably, not appearing to mind the lack of penitence in Leigh Benedict's tone.

'Mercutio had the most wonderful legs in those tights,' Anna put in, her clear, carrying voice sounding sharply in the silent street. 'And you wouldn't have been completely bored, darling. Juliet was a pretty little thing; she'd have kept you from falling asleep.'

Unable to suppress her feelings of annoyance and resentment, Jassy had been about to move away and wait for her friends at the far corner of the street, but the mention of Juliet stilled her and she listened to the rest of the conversation unashamedly. The old saying that eavesdroppers never heard any good of themselves slid into her mind, but she pushed it away firmly, curiosity getting the better of her.

'Actually, Juliet's rather special,' Benjy was saying. 'I would have liked you to meet her, Leigh.'

'Heaven, spare me, Benjy!' Leigh Benedict groaned. 'The last time you introduced me to one of your leading ladies it took me three months to disentangle myself from her clutches! I've had my fill of seductive little sirens who are so desperate to get on that they've practically got their clothes off before they say hello.'

'That sounds like my Gemma,' Benjy agreed with a rueful laugh. 'But this girl's different. She's got talent—and, unlike Gemma Morgan and her type, she's quiet, hard-working, and really rather shy.'

'She sounds painfully naïve.' Anna gave her words a harsh mocking intonation that grated on Jassy's raw nerves. 'And you were going to let

Leigh loose on the poor creature! Benjy, you're too cruel—he eats children like that for breakfast! She'll not last long if she's really the innocent you make her out to be—will she, darling?' She turned an intimate, smiling glance on Leigh.

'Don't be so cynical, Anna,' Benjy remonstrated. 'You saw her; she can act—and I find her innocence, as you call it, refreshing. There are too many Gemma Morgans in this world already.'

The three of them had come down the steps and on to the pavement, Anna still curved seductively against Leigh's side, his arm resting around her waist, and as Jassy moved even further back against the wall she could not miss the cynical twist to the actor's mouth as he spoke again.

'Your little innocent will learn, Benjy,' he drawled lazily. 'Heaven help her, she'll have to. The acting world is a jungle full of preying animals, and the ones who start out with stars in their eyes sell their souls soon enough when they discover the truth—either that or they go under. When she finds out she's getting nowhere, your sweet Juliet will resort to Gemma Morgan tactics like the rest; they always do.'

In spite of her determination to remain hidden, Jassy was unable to control an involuntary angry movement, her hand itching to come up and wipe that sardonically knowing smile from Leigh Benedict's face. She suppressed it almost immediately, but the tiny gesture had caught Benjy's eye.

'Jassy!' he exclaimed as she tried to shrink even further into the shadows, cursing the way she had betrayed herself as he came towards her. 'I didn't know you were still here. You must come and meet Leigh and Anna.'

Meet Leigh and Anna! Jassy almost exploded at the thought. She didn't want to meet either of them, couldn't have found a word to say to Leigh Benedict even if he were God himself—which he clearly thought he was, she told herself bitterly, unwillingly acknowledging that part of her inner fury came from disillusionment at seeing the truth about this man whom she had so much admired— as an actor, at least.

'No, Benjy,' she protested faintly. 'I——'

'But why not, honeybun——?' Benjy was clearly taken aback.

'This is a first, isn't it, Leigh?' Anna's amused tones broke in. 'Someone's actually *reluctant* to meet you—usually the reaction is quite the opposite. This little Juliet must be a very rare bird.'

'A very rare bird indeed.'

Leigh Benedict's sardonically drawled agreement was the last straw, setting a spark to the smouldering resentment in Jassy's mind and making it flare into a raging flame. Benjy's bulky frame and the shadows that surrounded her hid her from Leigh and Anna, and that fact gave her a glorious sense of freedom that loosed her precarious grip on her tongue.

'I don't want to meet your *friends*,' she declared, her voice high and tight, a cynical emphasis on the last word. 'I thought Mr Benedict came here as an actor, to offer constructive criticism and advice, but as he hasn't even seen my performance there's nothing he can say that I could possibly want to hear—and I can think of no other reason why I should want to talk to him. Leigh Benedict is not my type at all,' she rushed on thoughtlessly. 'I think his appeal is distinctly overrated! His publicity agents may claim that every woman in the country would put him at the very top of any list of the ten most sexually attractive men in the world, but he'd come way down on my personal rating—in fact, I doubt if he'd even be on it!'

The sudden silence that greeted her outburst brought her down to earth with a jarring bump. Benjy was staring at her as if she had suddenly gone completely mad before his eyes—which, in his opinion, she supposed she had, she reflected wryly. Leigh Benedict was a very powerful force in the film and theatre world; to antagonise him like this was a distinctly unwise move, possibly professional suicide, but she didn't care. The memory of the way he had implied that any young actress would willingly sell herself in order to achieve success made her blood feel as if it were boiling in her veins.

'And for your information, Mr Benedict——' she raised her voice, using all her training to project it clearly to where he stood '—here is one actress who isn't prepared to use her body to get the parts she wants. I intend to make a success of my career—but by my own efforts and ability, not by any other means!'

Luckily at that moment Sarah's car drew up beside her and Jassy hurriedly opened the door and clambered in, suddenly finding herself shaking all over in reaction to what had happened as the realisation of just what she'd said hit home. The last thing she heard through the car's open window was Leigh Benedict's voice, indolently cynical and with a thread of amused disbelief running through it.

'A *very* rare bird indeed.'

All the way home Jassy raged inwardly at the thought of the arrogance and selfishness of a man who had spent the day lazing on a beach somewhere without a thought for the effort, energy and time that had gone into the performance he had so callously not condescended to honour with his presence. Probably, as Louisa had said, he regarded such occasions as being beneath him now that he was a star. Her hurt pride eased slightly as she recalled Benjy's comment on her own part in the play, but any pleasure she might have taken in his words was tainted by the recollection of Leigh Benedict's cynical reaction.

The man was insufferable! He had implied that any girl who wanted to make her way in the acting world would be only too willing to sell herself to the highest bidder—and by that he probably meant himself. Jassy was suddenly intensely grateful for the fact that Leigh Benedict had not arrived in time to watch her performance. To have acted Juliet in all the glory and agony of her young love before this cynical, jaded man would, she felt, have been an act of sacrilege. Love would be just a word to him, something he had no understanding of, just as he had no understanding of idealism and integrity.

Well, she'd show him! Even if he wasn't aware of it—because the likelihood of their ever meeting again was slim, to say the least—she was even more determined than ever before to stick to her principles. She would sink or swim by her own efforts and never, ever resort to the sort of tactics Leigh Benedict seemed to expect.

And now, over two years later, she was still sticking rigidly to the vow she had made, though at times she had reluctantly had to admit that experience had taught her that there had been more than just cynicism and a prejudiced view of the world behind Leigh Benedict's comments; there had been some degree of truth as well. In her brief experience of the acting world, as opposed to drama school, she had come up against more than one director who seemed to believe that the casting-couch system was alive and well, and who became openly hostile when she made it plain that she had no intention of going along with their suggestion of providing 'a small favour' in order to win the part she had auditioned for. Only the previous week she had lost a part which she had believed was hers when another actress, a girl who had been in her year at drama school, had snatched it from under her nose because, as she had scornfully declared afterwards, she 'hadn't behaved like some Victorian virgin' when the director had suggested they mix business with pleasure.

But admitting that there had been some truth in what Leigh Benedict had said and agreeing to work for him for two months were two very different things. What would happen if he recognised her, remembered her impetuous words which, with hindsight, Jassy admitted had been foolhardy and rash to say the least? Sarah, who knew the whole story of course, was distinctly sceptical on that point.

'Don't be a complete moron, Jasmine!' she exclaimed, using the full version of Jassy's name which she knew her friend detested to emphasise her point. 'So you stung his pride a bit, but it was years ago. He'd probably forgotten all about it by the next morning. Besides, he never even saw you. I didn't realise you were there at first, you were so well hidden behind Benjy. He won't know you from Adam—sorry, Eve,' she corrected herself with a grin. 'You've got to be practical—this job's well paid, and you need the money. You can't muddle through on a pittance from Social Security much longer. You'd be a fool to turn this down.'

All sorts of a fool, Jassy admitted. What other temporary secretarial job would still give her some contact with the world she loved? And she had to admit that being involved, even if only on the most mundane level, with *Valley of Destiny*, Leigh Benedict's latest film, his first as director, was an opportunity she found it hard to resist. If rumour spoke true, the film was destined to be one of the greatest popular and critical successes of the year, and it was already one of the most talked-about productions, creating excitement and speculation whenever it was mentioned.

'I'll go for the interview anyway,' she said, reluctant to commit herself further. At least the interview wasn't with Leigh Benedict himself, but with a Steve Carter, the actor's personal assistant, so it would give her an opportunity to test the ground, find out just what her position would be. Perhaps she wouldn't have to have much contact with Leigh Benedict after all.

By the time the interview took place the next morning, Jassy knew that, if it was offered, she was going to take the job. It was too valuable an opportunity to miss, and a quick check with Francesca confirmed that the likelihood of anything as interesting—indeed, anything at all—turning up was just about non-existent, as she was already stretched to the limit to find work for her regular girls.

Jassy's half-formed decision was reinforced by the fact that Steve Carter turned out to be the sort of person whose friendly manner put her at her ease at once. He was an attractive man too, in his early thirties, tall, with light brown hair, blue eyes, and an open, pleasant face. He had none of Leigh Benedict's dramatic good looks, but Jassy privately felt that she infinitely preferred his easy approachability to the condescending arrogance that came with the actor's rugged sexuality.

The interview itself was routine enough, Steve Carter checking Jassy's certificates and references and detailing her duties, which were much as Sarah had already described. But Jassy's interest quickened as he went on, 'And of course there'll be a fair bit of work involved with this film Leigh's planning to direct—if we ever find a female lead.'

'Is there some difficulty over that?' Jassy tried hard to keep her voice even. Steve knew that the secretarial work was only a second string to her bow, she'd had to admit that to explain why she hadn't worked in that field over the past couple of years, but she didn't want him to think that she was trying to use her present position as a stepping-stone to greater things. She needed this job—only that morning, a postal delivery consisting of the electricity and telephone bills had brought home to her how much she needed it— and she didn't want to make any false moves that might ruin her chances.

'You could say so.' Steve's tone was dry. 'It's turning into a repeat of the search for someone to play Scarlett in *Gone With the Wind*. Leigh has very definite ideas about the sort of woman he wants to play Clara and so far no one's suited him. *Valley of Destiny* is very important to him. He's been involved in every part of it—the idea's his, the script's his. He's put a great deal of himself into the project and I'm afraid that doesn't make him exactly easy to work with. Your only consolation is that if he drives you hard he'll drive himself ten times harder. Of course, you won't be seeing much of him at first. You'll mainly be working with me—Leigh's in Scotland, filming at the moment, and he'll be there at least till the end of the month.'

The wave of release that washed over Jassy was so intense that she barely caught herself in time to hold back a sigh of relief. As she and Steve had talked she had become more and more convinced that she wanted this job in spite of its obvious drawback in the shape of the man who was to be her employer, but now it seemed that even that was not going to be the problem she had anticipated. Leigh Benedict's absence was an unexpected bonus, and one that left her able to respond to Steve's next words with unconstrained enthusiasm.

'I'm used to Leigh, I've known him since we were kids, and he's always been a workaholic, but it's only fair to warn you. Just don't take it to heart if he roars at you—it isn't personal. If you learn to shrug it off, you'll manage fine—that is, if you still want the job.'

'When do I start?' Jassy said quickly.

'Tomorrow, if possible. Your office and mine are on the ground floor of Leigh's house.' Steve scribbled something on a piece of paper and held it out to her. 'This address, nine o'clock.'

The first few days of Jassy's new job passed in a flurry of learning the ropes, finding where everything was kept, and forcing her mind and fingers to remember their long unused skills of shorthand and typing, but after that the work itself proved no problem, other than conquering her distaste for some of the letters she had to answer.

The amount and content of Leigh Benedict's fan mail frankly amazed her. To some of his fans it seemed that Leigh was not just a man but a god, his films the only bright spark in their otherwise depressingly routine lives, and some of them poured out their heart to him in a way that was almost unbelievable. The prying personal questions in some of the letters shocked Jassy, giving her a disturbing insight into the invasion of privacy that resulted from her employer's superstar status, and replying to them took a particular sort of tact in order to avoid their becoming a positive nuisance. She was well aware of the fact that it was just this sort of public exposure that had been one of her parents' major objections to her own desire to take up acting. So often, they had seen the private lives of popular stars plastered across the front pages of newspapers, and they had dreaded anything similar happening to her—something which would have caused waves of shock to reverberate round the small village where her father was the local GP.

How did Leigh Benedict cope with living in the glare of the spotlight as he did? she wondered, privately doubting that he would have any trouble adapting to the insatiable curiosity about his every movement. In every interview she had seen he had exuded an aura of total self-confidence, handling reporters and photographers with an easy, relaxed charm, accepting their attentions with the air of a man who had never known a moment's insecurity in his life.

The fan mail was the bulk of the correspondence, but there were other, official letters on matters of business that Jassy consulted Steve about, and a few personal ones that she put on one side for forwarding to Leigh in Scotland, but she was unsure how to proceed when, sorting through one morning's batch of post, she came across a letter addressed to Leigh with the name of a children's home stamped on the back.

'What do I do with this?' she asked Steve. 'Is it business or personal?'

Steve held out his hand for the letter, glancing briefly at the address on the back. 'Oh, Pinehurst again,' he said, clearly familiar with the name. 'Leave it with me and I'll see that Leigh gets it.'

He pocketed the letter and Jassy heard no more about it. When a second letter arrived from the same address she passed it on to Steve without comment, though deep inside she couldn't suppress a feeling of intrigued curiosity, wondering just what the connection between her employer and a suburban local authority children's home might be.

All this time Leigh Benedict himself was still away in Scotland and was expected to stay there for another two weeks; after that, he would be back in London to continue the search for an actress to play the role of Clara in *Valley of Destiny*. But, in spite of his physical absence, Jassy very soon came to realise that Steve had been telling the truth when he had said that the actor was not an easy man to work for.

Even though he was working day and night on one film, an endless stream of instructions about his next project were relayed to her through Steve, and from the first week she learned that the standards he set were very high indeed. But by the end of that week she was caught up in the job herself; the insights she gained into the production side of film work were rewarding enough to compensate for the demands her employer put on her time and energy, and she found an intense personal satisfaction in meeting every new command as swiftly and efficiently as possible. She rarely had time to think about her clash with Leigh Benedict two years before, but sometimes, when her mind wandered for a minute from the task in hand, she would remember those moments outside the drama college and a cold, apprehensive shiver would run through her at the thought that one day, before very long, she would have to come face to face with her employer.

When that happened she refused to allow herself to dwell on it, telling herself that what would be would be. Probably, as Sarah had said, he wouldn't even recognise her, and if he did— well, she'd handle that when it came.

Jassy and Steve soon fell into an easy routine in which she was the one who made the mid-morning cup of coffee, so she was in the stream-lined, ultra-modern kitchen one morning almost three weeks after she had started work when she heard the sound of a car drawing up outside, and a few minutes later the kitchen door opened abruptly and a tall, masculine figure strode into the room, halting abruptly as he registered her presence.

For a few confused seconds Jassy did not recognise him, her overall impression one of forceful vitality and an overpowering aura of physical strength. Then her gaze focused on a tangled mane of black hair, a heavy beard and moustache, and a pair of golden brown eyes that held her own so completely that for a moment she stood as if transfixed. But then the man spoke and the whole scene shifted, changed and took on a whole new meaning.

'Who the hell are you?' he demanded harshly, his tone making it only too plain that, whoever she was, she was not welcome.

From the first word Jassy's confusion vanished to be replaced by a shivering sense of apprehension as her stomach coiled into painful knots of near-panic. There was no mistaking that glorious voice, the one that had earned him the title of the new Richard Burton. Earlier than she had thought, her time had run out, the peace and quiet she had enjoyed was over, she acknowledged as, looking into those dark, hostile eyes, she saw past the misleading disguise of the dyed hair and beard and realised that she was face to face with Leigh Benedict.

CHAPTER TWO

'I SAID—who the hell are you?'

In spite of the warm summer sun streaming through the window, Jassy felt as if she had slipped back in time to a cool spring evening outside the college, as if she were twenty-one again, hearing that voice with its coolly cynical drawl from her hiding-place in the shadows, and the memory revived the angry feelings she had experienced then so that her own voice was cold and proud as she answered him.

'My name is Jassy Richardson,' she declared, feeling it was best to have that fact out in the open at once, her heart jolting inside her as she saw the slight flicker of response that crossed his face. Was that because Steve had told him her name as his new temporary secretary, or was he recalling where he had heard it over two years before, in a very different situation? Not for the first time she wished she had been called Mary or Anne, or anything that was more commonly used. 'I'm Mrs Eldon's replacement—from the Jobs Galore Agency.'

And right now she wished that Francesca *had* had jobs galore to offer her, so that she could have been anywhere but here.

'Ah, yes, the little secretary bird.' Leigh's indolent drawl had Jassy stiffening in indignation, warm colour washing her cheeks as she saw the blatantly assessing way his eyes roved over her face.

Her colour grew deeper as Leigh Benedict's gaze slid down over her tall, slender body, seeming to linger on the curves at breast and hip. Jassy felt naked under his obvious appraisal, as if he had stripped the clothes from her body with the intensity of his scrutiny. When he finally lifted his eyes to hers again she felt a tingling sense of shock and awareness shoot through her with the force of a powerful electric current as she saw the warmly sensual glow in those dark eyes, the slight, appreciative smile that curved the corners of an otherwise hard mouth.

Perhaps for many other women that smile would have seemed like the fulfilment of a dream, but, recalling his contemptuous dismissal of women in general, and actresses in particular, Jassy found that the only feelings it aroused in her were disgust and outrage, so that instead of looking away she stared right back, taking in his appearance fully for the first time without the shock of his sudden arrival clouding her eyes.

Leigh Benedict might give an impression of rugged sensuality in his films, but in fact he was not as broad and powerful as he appeared on the screen. In fact, his body was leanly built, that impression of strength coming from the firmly muscled lines of his chest and a pair of wide, straight shoulders around which a supple cream leather jacket clung like a second skin.

The black hair and beard were explained by the belated recollection that, as Steve had told her, Leigh's current role was that of a gypsy horse thief which had necessitated his growing and dyeing his blond hair. His fans were going to be bitterly disappointed, she reflected with a touch of irony. There was no sign of the golden mane or the strong-boned jaw that drove so many of them into ecstasies—but his eyes, of course, remained the same. Even in someone of only average good looks, those eyes would be stunning enough to cause a few female hearts to flutter. Clear and wide-set, their rich deep brown flecked with startling gold, and fringed with long, thick lashes, they were what drew and held her unwilling gaze.

Leigh Benedict was a spectacularly handsome creature, Jassy admitted reluctantly. There was nothing in the least boyish about him; he was a mature, virile character with an air of assurance that spoke of a worldly experience that would show in the lines etched around his nose and mouth if the heavy beard hadn't hidden them. The fan mail she had read had told her that few women felt that those lines in any way spoilt his looks—in fact, for most of them they enhanced his appearance. All in all, Leigh Benedict was a rugged devil of a man with a hard, lithe body whose firmly muscled lines were set off to advantage by the cream leather jacket, worn with a tan-coloured shirt and dark brown trousers which seemed moulded on to long, lean legs.

If she had hoped to disconcert him by returning his scrutiny stare for stare, then she had failed, Jassy admitted when the actor appeared not in the least disturbed by her defiant silence. But then, of course, Leigh Benedict was used to being the centre of attention. He thrived on it; in fact, he would probably be shocked if he was deprived of it. He had probably assumed that her own reaction had been one of the open adoration he was so accustomed to receiving.

Anxious to have that impression erased from his mind, Jassy rushed into unguarded speech. 'Could I have my body back now?' she enquired coolly. 'If you've finished with it, that is.'

That made his mouth twitch in a response that could have been anger, but then again might simply have been amusement, and Jassy was forced to regret her deliberately provocative remark as he responded silkily, 'As a matter of fact, no, I haven't finished. I'd like to take matters very much further.'

Once more those topaz eyes slid down her body, the curl at the corners of his mouth growing deeper as he caught Jassy's indignantly indrawn breath.

'You have a singularly attractive body, Miss Richardson, as I'm sure you're well aware, so I have to admit to being somewhat at a loss to understand why you seem determined to conceal its appeal under those appalling clothes.'

Leigh's description of himself as being at a loss was so blatantly untrue—he looked anything but, totally at ease and infuriatingly sure of himself— that his carefully assumed self-deprecatory tone added fuel to the fires of Jassy's anger so that she drew herself up stiffly, her grey eyes black with anger.

The role of secretary had taxed her limited wardrobe severely, the jeans and casual shirts that were perfectly suitable for rehearsals in huge, dusty, and often unheated theatres being completely inappropriate to her current position, so that she had been hard-pressed to find the right sort of things to wear. The problem had been compounded by the fact that she had wanted to choose clothes that, should she and Leigh Benedict ever meet, would project a mature, responsible and very conventional image to her employer, and so, hopefully, avoid awakening any memories of a casually dressed drama student he had once encountered.

It now seemed that she had succeeded in her aim. In fact, it appeared that she had succeeded only too well, she reflected rather ruefully, seeing the contemptuous distaste in those golden eyes as they flicked over her slightly old-fashioned grey cotton suit and neat white blouse. But then, of course, his taste inclined towards a rather more flamboyantly sexual style of female dressing, she acknowledged, recalling Anna Golden's dramatic appearance. *That* was not Jassy's style at all, though it was impossible to suppress a prick of very feminine pique at the way Leigh's mouth had twisted when he'd looked at her.

'I dress to please myself, Mr Benedict!' she snapped. 'I hardly think my appearance is any concern of yours. Did you object to the clothes Mrs Eldon wore, too?'

Her tartness was a mistake. She knew that as she saw his head go back slightly in response to her sharp tone. It might remind him of her outburst outside the college. So far he had shown no sign of connecting her with that incident, but if she didn't get a grip on herself she might revive memories which she would do better to try and leave buried.

Leigh's shake of his head sent his dark mane flying and a sudden, wicked grin made his teeth flash whitely against his tanned skin. 'No,' he murmured, so softly that instinctively Jassy tensed, suspecting strongly that he wasn't going to leave it at that, 'but then, of course, Mrs Eldon is nearing retirement age, and is very much the strait-laced schoolmistress type—she doesn't just dress as if she was.'

Without warning he reached out a hand and touched her hair, tugging one pale strand of it free from the neat chignon in which she wore it, and letting it curl around one long finger, his eyes glinting with a disturbing fire. Jassy froze, stunned by the total unexpectedness of the gesture.

'Pale hair, pale eyes.' Leigh's voice was a disturbingly husky whisper, one that made Jassy's nerves twist in instinctive response even as she tried to tell herself that this was just the tone he had used in the sensual love scenes in his last film. 'You look like some ice maiden in a fairy-story. What a terrible crime to have hair this beautiful and then drag it back in that unflattering style.'

'I . . .' Jassy began, but the words died in her throat as, with one hand behind her head, the pressure of his strong fingers at the nape of her neck gentle but irresistible, Leigh drew her face slowly and inexorably towards his.

His kiss was warm and slow, sensually exploring her lips with an expertise that she had never experienced before. Part of Jassy's mind wanted desperately to break free, get away, but another, less rational side to her brain seemed to be controlling her body, so instead she found herself doing quite the opposite, instinctively leaning nearer, the warm scent of Leigh Benedict's body filling her nostrils and a drowsy, glowing sensation flooding her veins, drugging her senses so that she couldn't think straight.

'Not so much of the ice maiden, after all,' Leigh murmured against her mouth, and his words were like the shock of cold water in Jassy's face, jolting her mind back into action so that she wrenched herself free, one hand flying up to her flushed face.

'How dare you?' she exclaimed furiously, struggling to meet those tawny eyes which were regarding her with a mixture of cynical amusement and frank disbelief. 'You had no right to do that!'

'You didn't exactly pull away,' Leigh pointed out with infuriating reasonableness.

'That doesn't mean I was enjoying it!'

Leigh's mouth twisted again, this time in a way that sent a *frisson* of cold discomfort through Jassy's body. 'Don't kid yourself, sweetheart. I hate to sound like some clichéd film script, but I do know when a woman's responding and when she's not—and you were definitely not fighting me off.'

'That's not true! I—I . . .'

The words died on Jassy's lips as the amusement in Leigh's eyes changed swiftly to dark contempt. She shook her head dazedly, unable to understand why she had been so disturbed by one kiss. It wasn't as if she'd never been kissed before! And it wasn't the fact that Leigh Benedict was a stranger to her, a man she despised and disliked, that had worried her. During her training, and on stage, she had had to kiss complete strangers and men she didn't like often enough not to let that bother her. But that had been acting, playing the part of someone else, not as herself.

Nor had it been the way Leigh's kiss had been deliberately calculated to arouse, holding a sensual invitation unknown in all the light-hearted romantic attachments she had experienced that had made her turn on him in this way. The real shock had come from the realisation that his cold calculation had worked only too well. She had been aroused in a way she had never known before and, if she admitted the truth to herself, until she had heard him speak she had thoroughly enjoyed the experience. It had been exactly what she wanted, so much so that the sardonically murmured comment, its cool tones indicating painfully clearly that Leigh had felt none of the heady response that had surged through her, had brought her down to earth with a shattering bump.

Leigh Benedict was watching her closely; Jassy sensed his tawny eyes on her face as she drew herself up stiffly.

'If you wanted to see Steve, he's in his office,' she said coldly, exerting every ounce of control she possessed over her voice so that it came out clipped and curt.

'Heaven help us, the ice maiden act again,' Leigh drawled mockingly. 'But it doesn't have quite the same effect any more,' he added as he turned towards the door. 'We both know you're not really Mrs Eldon's type, even if you try very hard to pretend to be.'

Believing him to be on his way out of the room, Jassy brought her teeth down hard on her lower lip to bite back the angry retort she was strongly tempted to flash at him. Just another minute, she told herself. Just sixty seconds and he would be gone...

But then, to her consternation, Leigh Benedict paused in the doorway and swung round to face her once more. 'Some other time, when I'm not quite so busy, we must continue this interesting— conversation,' he said in a voice that was laced with satirical mockery. 'I'd be intrigued to know what you're really like—to discover the woman like underneath all that ice.'

Left alone, Jassy drew a long, tremulous breath, too stunned by that final comment to be able to think. Automatically she reached for the kettle, but found that her hands were shaking too much to be able to turn on the taps to fill it, and slammed it down again on the worktop, her fingers clenching tightly over the handle as she struggled with the whirling, conflicting emotions in her mind.

Why did she feel like this? How could she have let Leigh Benedict get to her so badly? She didn't even like the man, and yet from the moment he had walked into the room every nerve in her body had become hypersensitive to his very physical presence. His objectionable, arrogant behaviour had alienated her from the start, but at the same time there was something indefinable about him that excited as much as it unnerved her.

Jassy felt hot and then cold as she thought of the way Leigh had kissed her, recalling the heady sensations the touch of his lips had awoken— which was crazy, because she hadn't wanted him to kiss her. Rationally, she would have said that that was the last thing she wanted from him. But he had kissed her, and her reaction had been so very far from rational.

Shaking her head at her own foolishness, Jassy took another deep breath, feeling her racing pulse calm as she regained control. She had been caught off balance, disconcerted by Leigh Benedict's sudden appearance, particularly because she had been dreading this meeting ever since she had taken on the job. As a result, she had acted completely out of character. She would be better prepared the next time, and at least she had one thing to be thankful for—her employer had shown no sign of recognising her or remembering the incident on the night of the production of *Romeo and Juliet*.

The sound of Leigh Benedict's car driving away a short time later told Jassy that the unwelcome visitor had gone, so it was with an easy mind that she carried the mugs of coffee into Steve's office, knowing she would not have to face her employer again that morning. It was as they chatted casually over their drinks that Steve surprised her by asking suddenly, 'Are you doing anything tonight? If not, I wondered if you'd like to have dinner with me.'

Jassy considered. She liked Steve and it was some time since she had had an evening out. There was no man in her life at the moment, and her strained finances had made it impossible even to go along with Sarah and her current boyfriend when they went for a drink at the local pub. And perhaps a night spent in Steve's pleasant, undemanding company would restore her sense of balance, erase the memory of a pair of mocking gold-flecked eyes, a cynically taunting voice.

'What a lovely idea! I'd like that very much.'

'I'm afraid I have a confession to make,' Steve said as Jassy finished her meal and leaned back with a sigh of contentment. 'This evening wasn't purely for pleasure—though I've enjoyed your company very much. I have to admit to having an ulterior motive.'

'Oh?' Jassy was intrigued. 'What was that?'

'I wanted to ask if you'd mind putting in a bit of overtime this weekend.'

'Overtime?' Jassy echoed the word because it was so unexpected. 'But of course I will! You didn't have to take me out to dinner just to ask that.'

'Ah, well——' to Jassy's astonishment Steve looked vaguely embarrassed '—this isn't exactly routine overtime—it would involve your staying at Leigh's house overnight. Look, let me explain. Leigh's due back this weekend—for once, filming's finished earlier than expected—and, knowing him, he's going to go hell for leather into work on *Valley of Destiny*—there are some script changes he's planning, for one thing. He's rewritten the damn thing three times, but he's still not satisfied. He'll want to get down to it straight away, so we'll need you on Saturday morning if that's possible.'

'I can manage that easily. But I don't quite understand. Why can't I just come in on Saturday? I don't see why I have to stay the night.'

'That's another complication. Leigh's driving down from Scotland on Friday night. Now usually there's a housekeeper who comes in when he's been away and gets the house ready, cooks a meal, that sort of thing. But I didn't expect Leigh back until next week so I gave her some time off. She's gone to see her daughter in Cornwall and won't be back until Monday. So——'

'You want me to take the housekeeper's place,' Jassy finished for him, and Steve nodded.

'I can't be around myself. I have to go to Jersey on Friday to check on a house we plan to use for filming, and I'll be gone all weekend. I can't say what time Leigh will arrive, he's not sure when he'll get away himself, but I don't expect it will be till late. That's why I suggested you stay at the house overnight.'

'Won't Mr Benedict object to my staying there?' Jassy asked, trying to gain time in which to think.

After her confrontation with her employer that afternoon she had been forced to reconsider her position and had come to the conclusion that her earlier inclination to refuse this job had, after all, been the right one—but not for the reasons she had originally believed. Earlier she had simply detested Leigh Benedict's cynical attitude towards up-and-coming young actresses, believing it was just actresses who were the object of his contempt. From the way he had behaved earlier she was now coming to the conclusion that it was women in general that he felt that way about.

'Oh, no. As a matter of fact, Leigh was the one who first came up with the idea.'

Jassy's eyes widened until they were soft grey pools of shock. *That* she hadn't expected. Just what had been in Leigh Benedict's mind when he had made that suggestion? The memory of his final declaration, 'I'd be intrigued to know what you're really like—to discover the woman like underneath all that ice,' had her opening her mouth in a rush to declare that the office overtime on Saturday she could manage, but the rest of Steve's request was impossible.

But Steve forestalled her.

'Leigh's perfectly capable of driving all that way after a day's filming and launching straight into work without any break, even for food, so I need someone who'll keep him on the straight and narrow, make him see sense, rest—eat.' His eyes had darkened with the sort of appeal that anyone would have found hard to resist. 'This really would be the most tremendous help to me, Jassy.'

The rain lashed against the window-pane with a fury that seemed to threaten to shatter the glass, and Jassy shivered slightly, feeling the chill in the air after the heavy heat of the day. The storm had broken early in the evening, not long after Steve had driven away on his trip to Jersey, leaving Jassy alone in the house—to wait for Leigh Benedict.

She still didn't know quite why she had overcome her misgivings and agreed to this when it was the last thing she wanted to be doing. She was being handsomely paid for her time, of course, and the money would be very welcome, but she would willingly trade that extra cash for a quiet night in her flat—preferably with a script to study.

But that was a forlorn hope. Only that morning she had phoned her agent, praying that some chance of an audition had turned up, only to have her hopes dashed.

'Nothing doing, I'm afraid, Jassy. Try again next week. If anything crops up in the meantime I'll let you know.'

So now she was here, completely at a loose end, with only the prospect of a meeting with her employer—something she was not looking forward to at all—ahead of her. She had unpacked her overnight bag, prepared a meal that would not spoil no matter what time Leigh put in an appearance, and had no idea what to do with herself next.

She had never been in this part of the house before, and the luxury of the room in which she was sitting, so unlike her own small, shabby flat or her parents' comfortable, rather old-fashioned home, made her feel distinctly ill at ease. She felt thoroughly out of place in the well-worn denim jeans and bright pink shirt she had changed into earlier. She wasn't here as Leigh Benedict's secretary, she had told herself. She was doing him, or rather, Steve, a favour, so she might as well be comfortable.

But comfortable was the last thing she felt. Everything around her was ultra-modern and undeniably expensive, but the long room with its stark white walls, thick grey carpet and black leather settee and armchairs seemed unlived in somehow, soulless, more like a showroom than a home. It had none of the personal touches that stamped a place with the personality of its owner, as if Leigh simply used the house as somewhere to eat and sleep—and work—and the rest of his life was lived elsewhere. Steve had told her that the entire place had been put in the hands of a currently fashionable interior designer, and, while she recognised Max Allen's style in the sleek, uncluttered lines of every room, there was nothing there to give her any clue about Leigh Benedict himself, nothing to help her.

Because she needed some help, Jassy admitted to herself. She had to talk to the wretched man about something. She couldn't just serve up the meal and spend the rest of the evening in stony silence, even if she would personally find that the easiest way out, knowing that she would have to keep a strong grip on herself in order not to let her personal feelings slip out. Acting, of course, was forbidden ground if she wanted to avoid sparking off a volcanic explosion when he remembered her foolhardy, impetuous comments over two years before—so what *could* she talk about?

There was little enough to go on in the publicity material she had worked on with Steve. All that told her was that both Leigh's parents were dead, when or how she didn't know, and he had no other family. He had trained at the same drama school Jassy herself had attended, but that was hardly something she would want to risk mentioning. Other than that there was nothing, just a list of productions he had appeared in and, of course, the seemingly endless array of awards.

The sound of a car door slamming outside interrupted Jassy's thoughts, bringing her hastily to her feet. It was such a dreadful night—he would welcome a hot drink straight away.

As she reached for the milk to pour it into a jug the kitchen door swung open and Jassy's hand jerked involuntarily as unconsciously she stiffened in apprehension. She couldn't look round yet, she thought, struggling against the memories of their previous meeting in exactly the same place that flooded into her mind. She couldn't face those tawny eyes until she was calmer, so she sensed rather than saw how Leigh paused just inside the room.

'Do you spend all your time making coffee?' The softly drawled mockery in his voice set Jassy's teeth on edge. 'Or do you just have a knack for knowing when I'm due to arrive?'

Or have you been sitting on tenterhooks just waiting for me to turn up? The implication was clear to Jassy, infuriating her, all the more so because that was exactly what she *had* been doing, if not quite for the reasons he believed. Exasperated, she swung round on him.

'Don't be ridiculous! I——'

The words died on her lips as her breath exploded in a shocked gasp. She knew she was staring, but she couldn't help it, couldn't drag her eyes away from the man before her.

She had expected the dark gypsy who had confronted her a few days before, but this man was so very different. The height and strong build were the same, he even wore the same cream leather jacket, now heavily spattered with rain, the white shirt underneath it soaked through and clinging to his chest where he had left the jacket carelessly unzipped. But he was clean-shaven and the firm mouth, no longer half hidden by the heavy black beard, looked harder, faintly cruel, the muscles in his jaw tense as if he was imposing a strong control over his uncertain temper.

Above that uncompromising mouth the tawny eyes were watching Jassy intently, noting every fleeting expression that crossed her face. She hadn't forgotten those eyes—their arrogantly appraising expression under heavy lids was one she remembered only too clearly. But the thick hair, slightly flattened against his forehead by the driving rain, no longer hung in an overlong mane almost to his shoulders. Even the effects of the wind and the rain could not disguise the fact that it had been carefully and expertly styled, and, although darkened by its drenching during the walk across the courtyard, it was very definitely not black but the bright golden blond that had helped earn Leigh Benedict his nickname.

Jassy had a sudden vivid image of all the newspaper and magazine photographs she had ever seen of this man, photographs that she now realised had, like the brief glimpse of him she had had over two years before, given only the vaguest impression of the full physical impact of Leigh Benedict's stunning good looks.

'The Golden Thief!'

Without meaning to, she had spoken the words out loud, and as soon as she heard her own voice she wished them back again, knowing they were a mistake as Leigh Benedict's face darkened, a ferocious scowl distorting his handsome features.

'So you read the gossip columns,' he commented savagely. 'Well, why stop there? What about "The Man Who Stole Anna Golden"? Surely you know that one too? Or have the gutter Press coined a new name—one I haven't heard yet?'

The cold, hard voice penetrated the haze in Jassy's mind, bringing her back to an awareness of herself and where she was.

'I'm—sorry,' she stammered. 'But I didn't expect—your hair——'

Leigh Benedict gave a short, harsh laugh, raking one hand roughly through his wet hair so that drops of rainwater from it spattered Jassy's face.

'Perhaps I should have left it black—you seemed to be able to find plenty to say to me then,' he muttered, the sardonic inflection in his voice making Jassy draw herself up hastily.

'I'm not taking back anything I said then,' she said stiffly. 'You——'

She broke off abruptly as Leigh sighed his exasperation.

'Heaven spare me! Not the ice maiden act again! Why do you pretend to be someone you're not? I know there's a real woman underneath it all, remember?'

Jassy's heart seemed to lurch inside her. She didn't want to be reminded of that particular incident. Since the time he had kissed her, here, in the kitchen, she had tried to erase the scene from her mind—unsuccessfully, she had to admit, remembering how thoughts of that kiss and the feelings it had aroused had crept insidiously into her mind no matter how hard she'd tried to force them away. More especially, she didn't want to recall those feelings now, when she had to be alone with him in his house for the rest of the night.

'I don't choose to remember that,' she said tightly, her inner turmoil making the words come out in a cold, hard voice that was quite unlike her own.

'You don't choose to remember,' Leigh echoed with such an uncannily accurate mimicry of her tone that, in spite of herself, Jassy admitted privately to a swift rush of admiration. 'But I do. I remember it very clearly. It's not something I'm likely to forget in a hurry.' Those gold-flecked eyes warmed suddenly, disturbingly. 'In fact, it's something I'd like to repeat.'

The gleam in his eyes warned Jassy, and as he took a step towards her she swung away sharply, moving swiftly across the kitchen.

'Well, I certainly wouldn't,' she said as coolly as she could from the comparative safety of the other side of the room, cursing the unevenness in her tone that gave too much away.

Leigh's movement, bringing him so much closer to her, had brought home to her forcefully that, for all his lean build, he still possessed a whipcord strength that was unnervingly imposing. Her sensitivity to his physical presence disturbed her, making her feel small and strangely fragile in a way she was not at all used to. Under normal circumstances she was well able to handle any man she met; five years in London had taught her the knack of putting down unwanted advances without any trouble, but this man was different, and from the look in his eyes she strongly suspected that he was not one to take no for an answer easily.

But to her surprise Leigh simply smiled and then quite deliberately let his gaze wander over her face and body, giving a small, silent nod of satisfaction as he did so.

'I hardly recognised you—I never realised that a change of hairstyle could have so much effect,' he murmured softly, and with a small exclamation of shock Jassy lifted a hand to her hair, feeling the loose, pale blonde strands of it falling softly about her shoulders.

She had meant to pin it up earlier, but had completely forgotten, and anger flared in her mind as the look on Leigh's face told her just what interpretation he had put on that one small fact. His next words confirmed her suspicions.

'What happened to the schoolmistress image? I must admit I prefer the current look—*much* sexier. What brought about the change, I wonder?'

Jassy faced those mocking topaz eyes, her own grey ones flashing a fiery denial of his arrogant assumption.

'I told you before—I dress to please myself and no one else! Your meal's ready whenever you want it,' she added hastily, taking refuge in practical matters to avoid any further confrontation. 'Don't you think you should get out of those wet things before you eat?'

Leigh glanced down at his clothes as if only just becoming aware of the way the rain had soaked them, plastering his shirt against the firm lines of his chest. Even his brown cord trousers were wet, clinging damply to his long legs in a way that Jassy found very disturbing. Her suggestion that he change out of his damp clothes was not purely a practical one. Once she had noticed the hard, lean shape of his body, emphasised by the soaking material, she found she could not look away. She had never been so forcefully aware of the potent attraction of a man's body before, and she just wanted him out of the room for a few minutes to give her the chance to come to terms with these new and unwanted feelings.

'Perhaps you're right,' Leigh said slowly, one hand going to his golden hair, brushing back the heavy, damp strands that had fallen over his forehead. His hand came away wet and he regarded it with a rueful expression that was disconcertingly appealing, tugging at something deep inside Jassy.

'If you get changed, I'll have the food ready by the time you come down,' Jassy said briskly, moving to take cutlery from a drawer, feeling the need of action to defuse the sudden and inexplicable tension that had gripped her. 'Well—go on!' she added when he seemed to hesitate.

'Yes, ma'am!' Leigh responded with a swift and disturbingly boyish grin.

Jassy was shocked to find herself suddenly filled with a longing to grab a towel and rub that glorious blond hair dry herself, feeling the softness of it beneath her fingers. The sensation was so strong, so unexpected that it took her breath away, leaving her incapable of thought. Unconsciously she half turned back towards Leigh, but he had already gone, and with a strange mixture of intense relief and something worryingly close to regret she heard his footsteps mounting the stairs to his room.

The rain had ceased, the thunder dimmed to a low growling in the distance, by the time Jassy joined Leigh in the living-room after clearing away the remains of the meal, but the restless, unsettled feeling she had experienced earlier had her in its grip again, making her feel very ill at ease. It was something like the feeling she had experienced before her first day at drama college, but then she had been on the verge of something very important and exciting, something that had been going to change the course of her whole life. In her present situation, such feelings seemed totally inappropriate.

She found Leigh sprawled in one of the huge leather armchairs, the black sweatshirt and jeans he had changed into blending with its darkness and providing a sharp contrast to the bright colour of his hair which was highlighted by the glow of a table-lamp he had switched on nearby. A tumbler of whisky stood on the coffee-table at his side, and he had a file of papers open on his knee which he was studying closely, occasionally making some note in the margin of a page. A workaholic all right, Jassy reflected, remembering Steve's comments. It was almost eleven and yet Leigh seemed set for a long night's work. It seemed she need not have worried about how to talk to him after all, she told herself with a touch of irony. He hadn't even noticed her come into the room.

Leigh's long legs were stretched out in front of him so that she had to step over them as she moved to sit on the settee. Her movement disturbed him and he glanced up, frowning slightly as if, totally absorbed in what he was doing, he had forgotten her presence and was trying to remember who she was. Then his expression cleared.

'Would you like a drink?' he asked affably enough, getting to his feet. 'I'm sure you could do with one after all your efforts.'

'A Martini would be nice—with lemonade.'

Jassy thankfully accepted the glass he held out to her, relieved to see that the rigidly controlled aggression she had always sensed in him before seemed to have eased and he appeared relaxed and much more approachable. She sipped her drink slowly, the ice clinking against the side of the glass. Perhaps the alcohol would help to relax her too. She would welcome anything that would ease the prickling, jittery sensation that felt like pins and needles all over her body.

Leigh returned to his chair, stretching his arms lazily, drawing the dark sweatshirt taut over his straight shoulders, and sighed deeply, tiredly. 'I must thank you for helping out like this. That was an excellent meal.'

'It was no trouble,' Jassy said carefully. She had suddenly remembered that Leigh himself had suggested that she come here tonight, and that thought intensified the pins and needles almost unbearably. 'Cooking in your kitchen is heaven after the conditions in our flat. You have a beautiful home,' she went on hurriedly in an effort to maintain the conversation.

Leigh lifted his shoulders in an offhand shrug. 'It'll do,' he said dismissively. 'It suits the so-called image, anyway. I hope being here hasn't upset any plans you had for the weekend. I'm sure there must be someone you'd rather be with tonight.'

Jassy wished he would look away. That remark about his image had awoken disturbing echoes of her own outburst over two years before, and his tone had altered perceptibly on his last comments, becoming strangely intent in a way that, combined with the direct, probing force of those golden eyes, scrambled her thoughts in the most worrying way.

'Well, Steve's out of town.' She blurted out the first thing that came into her head, even if the relationship she was implying did not actually exist. Although he had told her several times how much he had enjoyed their evening together, Steve had not actually suggested another date.

Her words seemed to change Leigh's mood suddenly. The heavy lids hooded his eyes, hiding their expression, as he leaned forward and replaced his glass on the table with meticulous care.

'I had forgotten about Steve,' he said cryptically.

He turned his attention back to the papers in his lap once again, and Jassy's curiosity got the better of her.

'Is that the script of *Valley of Destiny*?' she asked diffidently, and at Leigh's silent nod of agreement a flame of interest lit up inside her. Over the past few weeks she had learned a lot about the business side of the actor's work, but this was the first time that she had had a chance to touch on the creative aspect that most concerned her. 'Steve said you've already rewritten it three times.'

Again came that silent nod. Damn the man! He was being infuriatingly unforthcoming!

'Why?' she persisted, then stumbled over her words as his eyes lifted from the page to rest speculatively on her face once more. 'I mean— why is this film so important to you?'

The expression that crossed Leigh's face was neither a smile nor a frown, but a disconcerting mixture of the two.

'I want it to be a success.'

'But surely that's inevitable?' Jassy couldn't erase the shock and surprise from her voice. Anything Leigh Benedict touched turned to gold, and his name on the credits of a film guaranteed that it would be a surefire box-office hit.

'That depends on what you define as success.'

For a moment Jassy stared at him in blank confusion, then, recalling the letters she had had to deal with, she suddenly felt she was beginning to understand what he meant.

'The Golden Thief,' she murmured, her intonation very different from the one she had used earlier.

Leigh nodded agreement, the muscles of his face taut, drawing his skin tightly across his cheekbones.

'The feminist movement is swift to condemn any hint of a woman being treated as a sex object. Quite rightly, they see it as humiliating and degrading, but what they don't appear to have considered is that a man might find the experience every bit as distasteful. I'm an actor; I've served my apprenticeship and I'm on my way to becoming a craftsman. I've been lucky—I'm successful—but success can be a two-edged sword.'

'Don't you enjoy your work?' Jassy's voice was uneven as she tried to adjust to these new and unexpected developments. Was this man who described himself in such modest terms the same person she had dismissed as arrogant and self-centred?

'Enjoy it?' Leigh repeated thoughtfully. 'The work, yes, and I try to give the best damn performance I can—but whatever I do I can't shake off that sex-symbol label.' His mouth twisted wryly. 'Being flavour of the month every month can get a bit stale. Look, before I left Scotland

I had an interview with a journalist from one of the major women's magazines——'

'It didn't go very well?' Jassy questioned, alerted by his tone.

'Well enough—in her opinion. I shall reserve judgement until I read what she writes about me. That's the trouble with reporters, they listen to every word you say— "Oh, yes, Mr Benedict, or may I call you Leigh? I'm sure our readers will find this fascinating."'

As he spoke Leigh unconsciously assumed a soft, breathless voice, making Jassy smile in delight, secretly enchanted by the way he slipped into a role without thinking, and envying the skill that made her believe, just for a moment, that even a man so blatantly masculine as Leigh Benedict had become that woman reporter. She could learn so much from this man!

'But then what they write bears no relation to anything I've said. They've got an image in their mind and that's what they feed the public, ignoring anything that doesn't fit—and heaven help you if you don't live up to it. This woman didn't want to know about my *work*—she was more interested in my love life, which is nobody's damn business but my own! You're a woman,' he went on abruptly, startling Jassy with his sudden change of tone. 'Is that really what interests you?'

Caught off guard, Jassy shook her head vehemently.

'It would bore me silly!' she declared. 'I'd want to know why you choose the roles you do, how you prepare for them, how much of yourself you put into them...'

Her voice faltered uncertainly as she saw the way Leigh's eyes were fixed on her face, making her suddenly aware that she was treading on very thin ice indeed.

'I've never been terribly interested in what the stars eat for breakfast, what music they like, what car they drive,' she added hastily, and with what she hoped was a convincing degree of airiness.

'Well, that's what they ask me about,' Leigh said with a grimace of distaste. 'Personally, I'd like to hope that what I do is much more interesting than who I am. That's why I'm taking a back seat on this new project—letting someone else be the star. I'm doing this for my personal satisfaction—and to prove a point.'

'But surely you've proved yourself to be more than just a sex symbol already?'

Honesty forced the comment from Jassy. Whatever she thought of this man—and the things he had said had thrown her opinions into confusion—she could never deny that he was a brilliant actor who deserved every bit of the critical acclaim he had had heaped on him.

'Have I?' The question came with disturbing speed and force.

'Well—yes—you've won an Oscar.'

'Two, to be precise,' Leigh amended expressionlessly.

He wasn't boasting, there was something in his tone that told Jassy that without any room for doubt. He sounded more as if he was dismissing his achievement, reducing it to something totally negligible. Jassy couldn't believe it. If she had won any award she felt sure it would delight her for the rest of her life.

'But didn't that give you personal satisfaction?'

'You're an actress, you tell me. Would it be the *awards* that brought you satisfaction?'

'I see what you mean.'

Jassy's own experience gave her the answer. Wasn't that how she felt, sometimes seeming only really to come alive on stage. Awards, success, even the applause at the end of a play were somehow extraneous to the act itself.

'It's the *acting* that counts, giving the very best performance you're capable of.' Unconsciously she echoed Leigh's own words. 'What matters is getting across what the author means— expanding on the words on the page, enhancing them. Sometimes when a performance ends it's like dying a little...'

His question had touched a spark in her, firing her enthusiasm, and she had answered it without hesitation, but it was only now, when the first rush of excitement had died, that his quietly spoken first sentence hit her with the force of an explosion so that she froze, gaping like a stranded fish.

'You're an actress,' he had said!

'You—you know!'

Leigh didn't bother to pretend he didn't know what she meant, but merely nodded, those bronze eyes dark and expressionless, unfathomable.

'I knew from the moment I saw you—or at least from the second I heard you speak. I caught only the briefest glimpse of your face that night, but voices are my stock in trade, after all.' A faintly ironic smile touched his beautifully shaped mouth. 'I could never forget you.'

Or the things she had said, Jassy reflected uneasily, colour flooding her cheeks at the memory. 'Then why did you let me stay? Why didn't you dismiss me on the spot?'

That was what she would have expected. Surely he wouldn't want her to work for him when she had been so deliberately insulting, had scorned him so openly in front of his friends? But then, from what he had said tonight, the reputation she had shown such contempt for meant little or nothing to him.

'I needed a secretary.' Leigh's tone was bland, no trace of emotion ruffling its smooth surface. 'And Steve assured me that you were very efficient. I'd seen that for myself too, in the speed and accuracy with which you dealt with everything I sent from Scotland. And...'

'And?' Jassy prompted when he paused.

Those tawny eyes regarded her steadily and something deep in them made her heart lurch nervously and wish her question unsaid.

'You intrigued me,' Leigh said softly.

Jassy expected him to continue, elaborate on his enigmatic comment, but instead he picked up his pen again, turning his attention back to the script he was working on, his attitude telling her only too clearly that as far as he was concerned the conversation was at an end and he wouldn't welcome any attempt to start it again.

But Jassy had plenty to think about, her mind full of conflicting feelings, uppermost of which was the fact that she had not expected this degree of integrity from Leigh. She had assumed—quite wrongly, it seemed—that he enjoyed the adulation and attention his fame brought him. Clearly there were facets of his character that he took care to keep hidden from the Press and the public, and she wondered how many more she had yet to discover.

He had answered her questions frankly and openly, which was not at all how she might have expected him to behave when she considered how she had insulted him to his face on the night of *Romeo and Juliet*. And that was something she now had to reconsider in the light of all Leigh had said. Her hasty assumptions had to be brought out and looked at in this new light, like clothes that had once been an especial favourite but now, examined more closely, could be seen to be outdated and ill-fitting.

'You intrigued me.' That cryptic remark sounded in her thoughts, the tone in which it had been spoken reminding her of the last, cynically drawled words she had heard Leigh Benedict speak over two years before when he had described her as a very rare bird indeed. Just what did Leigh think of her? And, more complicated, what did she now think of him?

Absorbed in her thoughts, Jassy had almost forgotten Leigh sitting silently in the chair opposite, but gradually she became aware that even the faint rustle of a page being turned had ceased. Curiously she turned her head and found that he had fallen asleep, his head slightly to one side with his cheek against the soft leather of the chair, his blond hair falling over his face.

What did she do now? Jassy simply sat and watched him for a moment, frozen by her own indecision. She couldn't make up her mind whether to let him sleep or try to wake him so that he could go to bed and rest properly. If the truth were told, she felt distinctly nervous at the prospect of disturbing him. With those fierce bronze eyes hidden under heavy lids, and his face relaxed, he did not look at all dangerous. Sleep had softened the harsh lines of his face, smoothing away the hard, cynical expression he wore when awake, and, looking at him now, Jassy admitted that if she had never seen him before she would have to acknowledge a strong pull of attraction, drawing her almost to the point of wanting to like him.

Asleep, Leigh Benedict was just a man, never an ordinary one, for his looks defied any such description, but a very human man whose tiredness had caught up with him so that he had drifted asleep with the ease of an exhausted child. But underneath this disturbingly defenceless creature asleep in the chair lay the other man, the one she had seen outside the drama college, and, recalling the indolent arrogance of that man, the jaded tone in which he had drawled the cynical comments that had so angered and disgusted her,

Jassy knew that this more youthful, vulnerable appearance was just an illusion. If she were to wake him then the real Leigh, the man she had so detested, would be back, and right now she was glad of a respite from having to be always on her guard against letting her true feelings show.

Leigh stirred slightly, murmuring softly in his sleep, and the file of papers on his knee slipped, threatening to fall and send a cascade of pages over the floor. Hastily Jassy got to her feet and eased the file from under his limp hand. Straightening the papers carefully, she put them on the coffee-table and then, to her complete consternation, found herself unable to move away again.

She was so near to Leigh that she could hear the soft sound of his breathing in the silent room, see the way his chest rose and fell, the occasional flicker of the long, thick eyelashes that lay like dark crescents against his skin. The rich golden hair glowed in the light of the lamp, reminding her of that incomprehensible longing to touch it that she had felt earlier. As if of its own volition her hand reached out tentatively until it rested lightly on Leigh's head, feeling the soft strands of hair slide under her fingertips. The slight contact was intoxicating, making her shiver involuntarily.

As if sensing her touch, Leigh stirred again, sighing faintly as he shifted position, and Jassy snatched her hand away as if she had been burned. Perversely, in spite of the fact that only minutes before she had been glad that Leigh was asleep, she now wanted him to wake. His deceptively vulnerable appearance, combined with her own alien urge to touch him, made her feel that she would be much safer if he were awake. Then his face would resume its hard, aloof expression, she would see the cold light in those gold-flecked eyes, and know her present mood for the fancy it was.

'Leigh,' she said slowly, her voice soft and hesitant.

There was no response from the silent figure in the chair; he was too deeply asleep to hear her. Impulsively Jassy sank down on the arm of the chair, moving nearer to him so that she could rouse him carefully, not daring to contemplate his possible reaction if he was startled into wakefulness.

'Leigh,' she tried again. 'Mr Benedict.'

The long lashes fluttered slightly, but Leigh did not open his eyes. Leaning forward, Jassy touched his shoulder, meaning only to shake him gently, but the feel of the hard muscle beneath the soft cotton of his sweatshirt affected her as swiftly and shockingly as the moment she had touched the silkiness of his hair, and to her horror her fingers tightened convulsively, exploring the strength beneath them.

Leigh Benedict's eyes snapped open, looking straight into Jassy's face with a wary, questioning expression, and Jassy froze, the force of that tawny gaze holding her as if mesmerised, still leaning half across him, her hand still on his shoulder. A moment later the wariness faded from his eyes to be replaced by a warmly sensual look that was almost a physical caress and his mouth curved into an unexpected smile.

'Well,' he murmured softly. 'What have we here?'

One long-fingered hand moved to Jassy's face, tracing the line of her cheekbone with infinite gentleness, then slid slowly down to her neck, holding her without the slightest effort when she made a small, half-hearted attempt to move away.

'This is a most unexpected pleasure,' Leigh drawled, still in that low, seductive voice, as he drew her face gently but irresistibly towards his.

Jassy's throat was painfully dry. She wanted desperately to speak, but no words would form in her mind. She knew that she should move away and stop this now, before he got the wrong idea entirely—if he hadn't already—but she couldn't find the strength to break free from that light but inexorable grip on the back of her neck, and, if she was strictly honest with herself, she wasn't at all sure she wanted to.

Leigh's lips brushed hers in a tantalisingly brief caress and she felt all trace of resistance seep from her, to be replaced by a warm, glowing sensation that flowed through her veins like the effect of some potent wine. She scarcely noticed as Leigh's free arm slid round her waist, gently pulling her down from her perch on the chair arm so that she was half sitting, half lying across him, her head against his chest. When Leigh's mouth touched hers for the second time in a slow, lingering exploration of her lips Jassy closed her eyes with a faint sigh, oblivious of anything beyond this moment of total abandonment to the exquisitely pleasurable sensations his kiss was awakening in her. Deep inside she felt as if she had never truly been kissed before, as if, like some modern Sleeping Beauty, this was the one caress she had been waiting for all her life.

Sensing her surrender, Leigh tightened his grip around her waist, pulling her even closer, and her arms crept up around his neck, a small, wordless sound of disappointment escaping her when his mouth left hers for a moment. She heard his soft laughter then her lips were captured again, this time in a fierce, bruising kiss that forced her mouth open beneath his, sending shock-waves of reaction burning through her as if the blood in her veins were on fire. Leigh's hands were against her back; Jassy could feel the warmth of his touch through the thin cotton of her blouse, and her own fingers clenched in his hair in response.

'Hell!'

Leigh's exclamation came huskily against Jassy's lips as she moved in his arms, pressing herself closer still, her hands shaking as they tangled in the thick silkiness of his hair. Still keeping one strong arm tight around her, Leigh's other hand moved to the front of her blouse, dealing swiftly with the small pearly buttons that fastened it, until his hand closed firm and warm over the creamy breast his impatient fingers had exposed.

A fiery sensation of pleasure such as she had never experienced in her life before shot through

Jassy, a pleasure so sharply powerful that it was almost like a shaft of pain, making her gasp aloud. The very intensity of it left her mind suddenly very clear so that she heard Leigh's voice with a stunning clarity.

'I know what *I* want, my lovely secretary, so, tell me—what is it you're after?'

At once all those memories, so close to the surface of her mind because she had been reviewing them earlier, came flooding into Jassy's thoughts as inside her head she heard that same rich-toned voice saying with dark cynicism, 'When she finds out she's getting nowhere, your sweet Juliet will resort to Gemma Morgan tactics like the rest; they always do.'

She started violently, twisting in Leigh's grasp. She didn't want this, she thought wildly, not with this man, and, finding that his grip on her had loosened slightly, she pushed violently away so that the force of her movement carried her, stumbling, halfway across the room to stand, her heart pounding painfully, with her back to him.

Behind her she could hear Leigh's uneven breathing, could almost feel those fierce tawny eyes burning into her as she pressed her fist up against her mouth, trying to crush down the anger and disgust that rose up inside her.

'I'd be intrigued to know what you're really like—to discover the woman like underneath all that ice,' he had said, and he had done just that. She could have no doubt that what had happened had meant anything to him beyond a purely sensual experience, a deliberate experiment, but

she had succumbed to an assault on her senses
every bit as calculated and unfeeling as the way
in which he had kissed her a few days before.
And what made matters far worse was the fact
that he probably believed that she had responded
to him because of who he was; he probably saw
her as just another like the Gemma Morgan he
had described so scathingly.

A harshly indrawn breath warned her that
Leigh had recovered from his surprise enough to
speak, and instinctively she tensed, nerving herself
for his anger.

'You teasing bitch!'

The words were spoken in a low, controlled
voice that was all the more frightening for the
lack of violence in it. Anger she had expected,
but not this icy coldness. Fearfully she kept her
back towards him, struggling for some degree of
control.

'No!' Jassy's response was tremulous, her voice
just a shaken whisper as reaction set in. She
couldn't believe the way she had behaved, anger
and disgust warring in her at the way she had let
this happen, the way she had responded to him,
making her head spin. 'I *wasn't* teasing! I——'

'No?' the hard voice behind her questioned
savagely. 'Then what do *you* call it? I wake up
to find you practically in my lap, and when I respond as any normal man would under the circumstances you freeze up like some frigid little
virgin. You were making all the moves, lady.
Surely you're not going to claim I was forcing
you?'

'No.' Jassy's voice was very low. There was no way she could claim he had used force, but violence could have been no more devastating than the cold-hearted expertise with which he had deliberately set out to arouse her.

Suddenly she swung round to him, her dishevelled hair tumbling around her pale face in which her eyes seemed huge and dark.

'But it wasn't what you think! I was only trying to wake you.'

The cynical lifting of one eyebrow almost destroyed what was left of her shattered self-control. She was painfully aware of the fact that she wasn't handling this at all well, which was strange. After all, it wasn't that long since she'd been in a slightly similar situation, having to explain to Andy, the man she'd been seeing, that she had no intention of going to bed with him, and then she had had no trouble getting her message across calmly and easily. But then Andy was not Leigh Benedict. He was everything this man was not, warm, considerate, and he openly admired and respected the women he worked with, his attitude light-years away from Leigh's cynical degrading opinion of 'seductive little sirens'.

When her mind threw at her the irrefutable fact that Andy had also never been able to arouse her, make her forget herself in the way Leigh had done with just one touch of his lips, her throat dried painfully so that she had to swallow hard before she could go on.

'You didn't look very comfortable,' she said awkwardly. 'I thought you'd be better off in bed.'

'With you?'

Jassy stared at the fine-boned face before her, seeing arrogance and contempt stamped clearly on the hard mouth, glittering in the golden eyes, and a hot wave of anger swept through her, driving away any thought of caution from her mind.

'You're so bloody conceited!' she stormed, shocking herself with her ferocity. She was over-reacting again, but this time she didn't care. Even the swift, ominous narrowing of Leigh's eyes was ignored as she gave vent to the feelings that had been stored up inside her since the night of *Romeo and Juliet*. 'You really think that just because you're Leigh Benedict—the damn Golden Thief—every woman you meet must be longing to get into your bed—that they'll lie down and let you trample all over them if you'll just spare them a minute of your precious time! Well, you've mis-judged things completely this time! Here's one woman who's totally indifferent to your much-vaunted charms. In fact, Mr Superstar Benedict, you make me sick!'

She had been right, Jassy told herself ruefully as the sound of her voice died away—right to have such strong doubts about taking this job, right to think that her anger and resentment at the things she had heard him say could not be kept in check when she and this man came face to face. There was a bitter taste in her mouth as she recalled how, such a short time earlier, she had come close to revising her opinion of Leigh Benedict, had admitted to some sympathy, even some admiration for him. The swift destruction of that fragile understanding had added fuel to the bitterness that had caused her final outburst.

She opened her mouth to speak again, though not really knowing what more she could say, but the slow, sardonic curl of Leigh's lips closed her throat.

'Is that so?' he said softly, his eyes mocking her pitilessly. 'Well, you'll have to forgive me if I don't exactly believe you. If that was indifference—or more—you have the damnedest way of showing it.'

The silkily spoken taunt brought a shaky gasp to Jassy's lips. Her anger deserted her just when she needed it most, and it took all her fast-dwindling reserves of strength to say anything.

'You took me by surprise. If I'd had time to think...'

Jassy's tightly controlled voice faltered beneath Leigh's steely gaze. That wasn't true—and he knew it, damn him! She squared her shoulders and, drawing herself up proudly, forced herself to look him straight in the face.

'But it won't happen again, do you understand? *Never!* I'm not available—certainly not to you!'

'Don't flatter yourself,' was the swift, uncomplimentary response. 'I'm not so desperate for female company that I'd choose to spend my time on some immature schoolgirl who doesn't know her own mind.'

Insulting as his words were, they were infinitely welcome to Jassy. If that was how he felt then surely she was safe from any repetition of what had happened? She felt the tension in her body ease, leaving her drained and exhausted.

But she had relaxed too soon. With a sudden lithe movement Leigh was out of his chair and had caught her arm in a painful grip, his other hand wrenching her chin up, forcing her eyes to meet the cold blaze of anger in his.

'But I warn you, I don't take too kindly to some juvenile Lolita using me to practise her wiles on. I reckon I owe you one, and I don't forget easily, so you remember that. Meanwhile, here's a little something on account——'

Before Jassy quite realised what Leigh intended she was pulled into his arms and he kissed her hard, a harsh, savage kiss that was more a bruising assault than any form of caress. He controlled her struggles with an easy indolence that belied the strength of his grasp, forcing her tight up against his body and holding her for just as long as he wanted before he released her so abruptly that she staggered backwards, one hand going automatically to her bruised mouth.

'I think that evens the score a little,' Leigh declared grimly.

He surveyed her dishevelled appearance coldly, his eyes, like chips of golden ice, lingering for a moment on the soft swell of her breasts still clearly visible beneath her unfastened blouse, before they flicked back up to her flushed face.

'Fasten yourself up,' he ordered brutally. 'I've seen quite enough of you for one night.'

And the appalling thing was that, even as the door swung to behind him, Jassy had to admit to herself that although that last kiss had been given in anger, meaning only to punish her and nothing more, it had stirred those unwanted longings deep within her just as surely as any of his earlier, more gentle caresses had done.

CHAPTER THREE

IF IT had been at all possible, Jassy would have left Leigh's house then and there and never come back, and to hell with her job, no matter how much she needed it. But it was well after midnight, she didn't have enough money in her purse for a taxi fare, and it would be the height of foolishness to risk making the long journey back to her flat alone at this time of night. So she had no alternative but to go to the room Steve had shown her, where she got into bed, but not to sleep.

Instead, she tossed and turned restlessly as her mind replayed over and over again the events of the evening like a film projected on a screen, never coming any nearer to a rational explanation for her own behaviour.

The response Leigh Benedict's coldly calculated caresses had awoken in her had had something of the same effect as being thrown into a swimming-pool at the deep end with only the vaguest idea of how to swim. Since she had come to London to study, and in the years since she had left drama college, her dedication to the idea of becoming an actress had been all that had motivated her, and the time and commitment that had been demanded had left her with little energy or inclination for any serious romantic attachments. Casual sexual relationships were not for her, the risks were too high, and besides, she had always believed that true physical fulfilment could only come from loving someone and knowing that they loved you. So she had always said no—and meant it—but there had never been any panic, any recrimination. She was able to call a halt with a word and a smile, ensuring there was no ill-feeling on either side.

But with Leigh Benedict her carefully thought-out approach had deserted her. As an actor, he commanded her respect and admiration, but as a man the feelings he aroused in her were exactly the opposite, and yet, in a few brief minutes, he had taught her more of what it really meant to be a woman than any other man she had ever met. He had brought her to a point at which she had had no thought of principles, or even the way she had decided was the best, she would have said the *only*, one for her. Leigh had somehow found the key that opened the door to her own personal sexuality, and, having had that door opened, Jassy knew she had to go through it. There was no way she could simply close it again and pretend she didn't know what lay on the other side.

But she would not go through it with Leigh. What had happened between them had meant nothing to him; he saw her only as one of the actresses he had described, believing her to be attracted by the aura of fame, power and influence he carried with him, and had treated her accordingly. The thought repelled her and in the cold light of dawn she came to a decision.

She would have to leave; there was no way she could work for Leigh now. She was not prepared to work for a man who despised her, however unjustly. She did not allow herself to consider how she might feel if she never saw Leigh again.

Fired with resolve, she made her way to her office the next morning. Her office no longer, she thought on a pang of regret. She had enjoyed her job, and in any other circumstances would have been happy to keep it—not least because the pay was good and she desperately needed the money. But Leigh gave her no chance to declare her intention of leaving, glancing up from the pile of papers on his own desk to wave a hand at a bundle of letters.

'See to those, will you?' he said with a casualness that astounded Jassy. 'I shall want to dictate some letters to you later.'

Jassy could only stand still and stare at him. This was not how she had expected the morning to go! A carefully formal speech of resignation was clear in her head, but somehow she couldn't bring herself to form the words she had practised over and over again.

Just to see Leigh had brought memories of the previous night rushing back into Jassy's mind, but he was behaving as if that night had never been, as if she had just arrived for work on an ordinary morning. Then her mind cleared. She had forgotten what a consummate actor Leigh was. He was a man who could turn on any emotion, or the lack of it, at the word of a director or, as he was doing now, for his own private reasons.

Well, she was an actress too, wasn't she? If she treated her position here simply as a part, a role she had to play, then perhaps she could hide last night's turmoil behind a mask as distant as his own and play the scene as Leigh directed.

'I take it you still want me to work for you?'

She recognised that voice; it came from her last part but one, when she had played a haughty French aristocrat during the Revolution—all that was missing was the accent.

'I expect you to work *with* me——' Leigh returned imperiously. 'We're going to be snowed under with paperwork for the next couple of weeks and I need someone I can rely on to work efficiently under pressure.'

Glancing up, he caught the slight change in her expression that she was unable to hide.

'I need a *secretary* more than ever.'

The emphasis on the single word couldn't be clearer, and it revived the feelings of outrage that had held her in their grip through the long, dark hours of the night. Now was the time to tell him just what he could do with his job.

'But . . .'

Her voice failed her as a smile tugged at the corners of that firm mouth. The smile told her everything and pulled out from under her feet her conviction that leaving was her only way out of this situation with her self-respect intact.

Leigh *expected* her to leave! If she walked out now it would confirm his cynical suspicions, his belief that the only reason she had come to work for him was because she had hoped to seduce him into using his influence in the acting world to help her a few steps up the career ladder. Handing in her resignation would only make him assume that he had been right in his interpretation of her behaviour last night and that, finding that her sexual tactics hadn't worked, she was leaving because there was nothing to be gained by staying.

She was caught in a cleft stick. She didn't want to stay, couldn't bear to think of working for this arrogant, self-centred devil, but her self-respect mattered more. She had declared to his face that she was one actress who wouldn't sell herself in order to get on, and if she was to convince Leigh of that—and suddenly convincing him of the truth had become much more important than anything else—then she had to stay.

'I'll get on with the post then,' she said crisply, every inch the perfect secretary—something which clearly had not escaped Leigh, as that lop-sided and singularly attractive smile, an infuriatingly irrational part of her brain acknowledged, tugged at his mobile mouth again.

'Do that,' he said drily.

The routine of opening, sorting, and answering the letters was by now so familiar to Jassy that the procedure soothed her jangled nerves and she was soon absorbed in the task, able to forget Leigh's disturbing silent presence temporarily at least. When Leigh did speak to her, his tone was strictly businesslike, with no hint of anything beyond the matter in hand to worry her. His behaviour was purely that of employer to employee, polite but uninvolved, and if he was to keep it that way she felt she might be able to cope with working for him after all.

Halfway through the morning the phone rang and Leigh answered it, firing questions swiftly at the person on the other end of the line and making brief notes on a pad in front of him.

'That was Steve,' he said a short time later when he had put the receiver down. 'He asked me to tell you he'll be back tomorrow.'

Leigh was watching her, waiting for her reaction in a way that made Jassy feel vaguely uneasy, and that feeling, combined with a sudden strong sense of relief at the thought that when Steve returned his cheerful personality would act as a buffer between herself and Leigh, made her over-react, putting more enthusiasm than was strictly necessary into her reply.

'That's great. I'll look forward to that,' she said brightly, then deliberately followed Leigh's own example and turned her attention firmly to her work, not waiting to see how he reacted.

There, she thought with a small sense of triumph, let him make what he wanted of that! With any luck he would think that she and Steve were rather more than just friends and, hopefully, that would make him keep his distance. Surely even Leigh Benedict would have the decency not to try anything with his friend's girl? When an inner, coldly realistic part of her mind reminded her that Leigh had made it plain that he had no intention of trying anything, that, on the contrary, he believed that *she* was the one who might make any move, she pushed the thought away hastily, forcing herself to concentrate on her work instead.

After lunch, when Leigh insisted that Jassy took the full hour she was entitled to though he spared himself only ten minutes away from his desk, the silence in the room began to feel oppressive. Jassy was used to having no one to talk to, having spent so many days alone in this room in the past few weeks, but this silence was constrained and unnatural and she longed for something to break it, so that when the telephone rang again she snatched at it swiftly, grateful for the interruption.

'Mrs Eldon?' The distinctively husky female voice at the other end of the line was instantly recognisable, especially as Jassy had heard it again so very recently, and her mind went back to the evening Steve had taken her out to dinner.

Anna Golden had been seated at another table in the restaurant, surrounded by a group of friends, the dramatic mane of red-gold hair falling halfway down her back instantly revealing her identity to Jassy. Glancing up, the actress had recognised Steve and had immediately got to her feet, heading towards their table.

Jassy had watched her come, her mind full of the last time she had seen the older woman, over two years before. Anna Golden was deeply tanned, her bronzed skin in strong contrast to the soft beige suede of the sleeveless trouser suit that plunged to a deep V over her voluptuously curved breasts. Gold chains glinted at her throat, a wide gold belt encircled her narrow waist and her already impressive height was emphasised by a pair of ridiculously high-heeled sandals. Jassy knew that the actress must be around forty, but she could have claimed to be ten years younger and got away with it. Her acting career might have been eclipsed by that of her younger, more successful lover, but as she swayed seductively across the room Anna Golden still clearly thought of herself as a star.

'Steve, darling!'

Her smile was obviously insincere, and Steve's in response was equally forced. Instinctively Jassy stiffened, feeling vibrations of dislike and distrust reach her as if on the air she breathed.

'Have you heard from Leigh when he's coming back from Scotland? Poor darling, he must be terribly lonely up there in the wilds. There's no civilisation for miles. But I'll make it up to him when he gets back. I'm planning a very special reunion—just the two of us, a quiet meal, and some excellent champagne.'

Steve gave a non-commital murmur, but Anna did not appear to need any reply.

'Give Leigh a message for me when you see him. Just tell him I'll be waiting for him—he'll understand.'

That purring voice was beginning to grate on Jassy's nerves, the breathy, caressing intonation making her feel positively sick. It seemed there was little difference between Anna Golden and all those adoring women whose letters she had been dealing with for weeks. But perhaps that was the way Leigh Benedict liked it.

'I know how strung up he is when he's finished filming, but I have my own special ways of making him unwind.'

'He'll be working hard when he gets back.'

Jassy was distracted from her private reflections on Anna's comment that Leigh would be 'strung up', something she personally understood only too well, by the evident constraint in Steve's voice.

'We're auditioning for the female lead in *Valley of Destiny* very soon.'

'Ah, yes, Leigh's precious film.' Anna's tone was tart. 'I should have thought he'd be desperately tired of dealing with young hopefuls by now. He'll be ready for some more—sophisticated company to take his mind off things.'

The actress stretched luxuriously like a contented cat, a sensual smile curling her lips as if at some private memory, her green eyes lighting with a lascivious gleam that was almost indecent in a public place. That smile was in Jassy's mind now, making her voice cool and distant as she spoke into the telephone receiver.

'Mrs Eldon's on sick leave, Miss Golden. I'm acting as secretary temporarily.'

'Oh, yes, Steve's little friend.' Anna Golden's tone implied that Jassy she had found all too easy to forget.

Out of the corner of her eye Jassy saw the way Leigh's head had lifted on hearing the caller's name, and now he was quite obviously listening to every word she said. A sudden wave of hot anger washed over her at the thought that, last night, Leigh had made his unjustified contempt of her so plain when his own slate wasn't exactly clean in such matters. His affair with Anna Golden had been responsible for the break-up of the actress's marriage, and yet he had had the nerve to be so contemptuous of her own behaviour and the motive he had ascribed to it.

'Anyway, it's Leigh I want to speak to. He is there, isn't he?'

Automatically Jassy glanced across at Leigh, questioning expression on her face as she held the telephone slightly towards him. She was frankly surprised by the moment's hesitation before he nodded in response to her unspoken enquiry.

'Yes, he's here,' she said to Anna. 'Just one moment.' She held out the receiver to Leigh as he came to take it from her.

'Anna——' Leigh's voice was urbane and good-humoured, the momentary hesitation apparently forgotten so that Jassy wondered if in fact she had imagined it '—when did you get back from Greece?'

With an effort Jassy directed her attention back to her work, struggling to ignore the lean body resting against her desk, one long-fingered hand lying casually on its top, very close to her typewriter. She didn't like Leigh, she told herself firmly. In fact, she positively detested him—but that thought did nothing to calm her pulse which had quickened in the most disconcerting way simply because of his nearness.

'Tonight?' Leigh was saying. 'That could be difficult. Oh, I see—well, I suppose I could manage that. I've a couple of things to sort out here, but I could be free later. After seven OK?'

Clearly the actress had planned that tonight would be the time for that 'very special reunion' Jassy reflected cynically. Though, strangely, Leigh did not appear as enthusiastic about the scheme as Anna's words had led her to expect. She supposed that that was because he resented anyone, even his mistress, interrupting the work on the film that he had made plain was so very important to him. She couldn't resist a small smile at the thought of Anna Golden's reaction to having to take second place to Leigh's work.

A moment later Leigh was laughing, a warm, relaxed sound that Jassy had not heard from him before. Involuntarily she glanced up to catch the smile on his face, that sudden, swift smile that changed him so dramatically, transforming his hard features, and an unexpected sharp pang shot through her at the thought that last night he had smiled at her like that, just once—but never again.

'Anna, you are incorrigible! That remark was definitely slanderous. Restrain your lurid imagination, you'll offend my new secretary's delicate sensibilities.'

Jassy started slightly at his reference to herself, and at that moment the tawny eyes swung round to her face. She was held transfixed by Leigh's mocking gaze, unable to look away when he spoke again.

'You've met her? When?'

As he listened to Anna's reply another smile curved Leigh's beautifully shaped mouth, but, unnervingly, Jassy noticed that this one did not reach his eyes. Deliberately he paused and let his gaze sweep over her, insolent and assessing in a way that brought hot colour rushing into her cheeks.

'No,' he drawled slowly, 'nothing like Mrs Eldon.'

Jassy's embarrassment fled before a wave of fiery anger at his words. How dared he discuss her with Anna Golden like this as if she weren't in the room? Biting her lower lip hard to keep back the furious outburst that almost escaped her, she reached for the letters in front of her and began sorting through them aimlessly. There was nothing more to be done with them, they were all finished and waiting for Leigh's signature, but she needed something—*anything*—to occupy her so that she didn't have to meet Leigh's eyes again.

Mercifully he put the phone down a few seconds later and silently held out his hand for the letters, glancing through them swiftly before he signed his name at the bottom of each page. Then, to Jassy's surprise, he read them all again, frowning thoughtfully as he did so.

'How did you learn to do this?' he asked suddenly. 'Mrs Eldon's been answering these things for years so she knows what I want, but you've hit exactly the right note straight away.'

Jassy did not know how to answer him. She had replied to the fan letters as she would have wanted them answered if she were in Leigh's position, trying to avoid obvious formula letters and yet, while showing appreciation of their interest, always being aware of the need for reticence in order to preserve some personal privacy.

'It's not always easy,' she said diffidently.

'I'm aware of that.' Leigh turned that disturbingly direct gaze on her once more. 'But they're part of the job. The people who write those letters helped to put me where I am, so the least I can do is answer them—but I'll not let myself be eaten alive because of that. Publicity's a fact of life in this business, but publicity for my work, Leigh Benedict the actor—everything else is quite irrelevant. You show an unusual understanding of that fact, and I couldn't have done better myself.'

'I tried to put myself in your place when I answered them,' Jassy murmured, torn between a desire to keep her distance as much as possible and a need to give in to the unexpected glow of pleasure his appreciative comments had sparked off inside her.

'That can't have been easy,' Leigh flashed back, reverting to his usual satirical character. 'You must have had to work damned hard to suppress your true feelings.'

Abruptly his expression changed, those bright eyes suddenly intent on Jassy's face so that instinctively she flinched away from the probing force of his gaze. She felt as if he was searching deep into her mind, trying to draw out her innermost thoughts.

'What sort of actress are you?' he demanded, throwing Jassy completely off balance mentally at this unexpected turn of the conversation into an area that felt perilously like a minefield.

'I——'

'Are you any good?'

How did she answer that? Professional pride gave her the confidence to meet his eyes. 'I had a couple of decent reviews, but I'm only just starting out.'

'What have you done?'

'Cecily in *The Importance Of Being Earnest*; Viola in *Twelfth Night*——' when compared with his own achievements it sounded so very little, so insignificant 'and I was Rosalie in *Moonrise*, but——' her smile was wry '—that didn't last very long.'

Leigh nodded slowly. 'I saw that—the play was appalling.'

Jassy felt as if someone had just punched her in the stomach, leaving her gasping for breath. *Leigh* had seen her performance as Rosalie! Irrationally, she felt that it was impossible that he had been in the audience and she hadn't known. Even disliking him as much as she did, she couldn't deny the forceful impact of his physical presence. Surely some sixth sense should have alerted her to the fact that he'd been in the theatre?

Then the memory of how much she had wanted his critical opinion of her abilities over two years before crept into her mind and it was impossible not to dwell on that cryptic 'the play was appalling' and wonder what he had thought of her performance. The question burned on her lips, but pride and a sudden strong sense of self-preservation forced it back.

She was here as Leigh's secretary, nothing more. He had made that only too plain. To ask his opinion of her performance could be interpreted as another attempt to use her position here to her own advantage, something she had vowed she would never let him do. But all the same, she wouldn't be human if she didn't wonder. *Had* there been the slightest emphasis on 'the *play*'? Could Leigh have meant to imply that *she* hadn't been as bad as the production?

But as her eyes went to Leigh's face in an attempt to try to read in it if there had been something else behind his words he moved away towards his desk to pick up a thick folder which he dumped unceremoniously down in front of her.

'That's the final draft. I've done all the alterations, now it just needs typing up—but I need it done quickly. Can you come in tomorrow?'

Jassy opened her mouth to speak, then hesitated. At the back of her mind warning bells were sounding faintly, woken as a result of Leigh's disturbing and unexpected questions. Could she really continue to work for him, knowing what he thought of her, or wouldn't it be wiser, safer, to tell him now that she was leaving and get out with some shred of pride left intact?

'Double time.' Leigh's voice sounded tautly in her ears.

But Jassy really wasn't listening. Still wrestling with her inability to make a decision, she had lifted the cover of the folder on the desk and what she saw underneath it made her draw in her breath sharply.

This was the script of *Valley of Destiny*, the production that had had the whole film world talking and speculating for months. Was she really going to turn down the chance to be a part, however lowly, of the team that worked on that film? Already there were rumours that it would be one of the biggest films of the year, if not the decade. This might be the only opportunity she would ever have to work on something so important.

'I can come in any time you want.' Jassy heard her own voice with something of a shock. She had spoken from the heart; rationally she still had not decided.

But the words had been said, there was no taking them back, and if she was honest she did not want to retract her agreement. Even typing out the script would add to her knowledge of the process of filming and she couldn't afford to pass up such a valuable chance. After today she would be well settled in to her role as Leigh's secretary, and if he continued to be as distant and aloof as he had been all day then she could put last night's events behind her and play that part as long as was necessary. Feeling more confident, she lifted her eyes to Leigh's.

'I'll do as much overtime as you need,' she said firmly.

'Fine.' Leigh's tone was crisp. 'I'd appreciate that.'

Unexpectedly he leaned towards her, resting his hands on the desktop, his nearness infinitely disturbing to her peace of mind.

'I really would appreciate it,' he said with a new and very different note in his voice. 'I realise what I'm asking. You've already given up more than half of your weekend to help me out. If you think I'm pushing you too hard you've only got to say.'

Jassy could hardly believe her ears. Such consideration was the last thing she had expected! But then she had forgotten that Leigh was playing the part of the perfect boss. It was a role he played particularly well too, she reflected satirically, recalling the bouquets of flowers she had sent, on Leigh's instructions, to the indisposed Mrs Eldon. He knew all he moves, all the gestures.

'No, it's all right, I can cope,' she said awkwardly as Leigh straightened up.

'Thanks,' Leigh said briefly, but the single word was accompanied by a smile so unforced and so unexpected that it took her breath away.

Even when he was back at his own desk she found that it still affected her, making her hands suddenly clumsy so that they hit all the wrong keys, making a terrible mess until she tore the paper from her typewriter in a fury of exasperation at the chaos she had made of a perfectly simple task.

Damn him, she thought to herself, flinging the crumpled sheet in the vague direction of the waste-paper basket, not caring that she missed it completely. Just when she thought she'd got things all sorted out and knew exactly where she stood with him, something like that had to happen, setting her pulse racing, bringing every nerve alive in the most unsettling way, and she was right back where she had started, thoroughly confused by her own reactions, and not at all sure that she liked what was happening to her.

With the typical unreliability of an English summer, the rain began to fall late in the afternoon, lightly at first, spattering the window with fine drops, then steadily increasing until it was a savage, torrential downpour. Jassy sighed faintly, thinking of her journey home, and Leigh glanced up, frowning as he looked out at the sodden garden.

'You can't go home in this,' he said, almost as if he had read her thoughts. 'If you can hang on till six-thirty I'll drive you home.'

'It doesn't matter,' Jassy answered hastily. 'I can get a bus.'

'You'd drown before you reached the bus-stop,' Leigh told her in a tone that brooked no further argument. 'I'll take you—I have to go out anyway.'

Yes, and she knew just where he was going. Jassy couldn't help wondering if he would have bothered to offer her a lift if he had not been going out already. Another gesture.

Just after six Leigh stretched lazily and got to his feet.

'You can pack up now,' he told Jassy. 'And get your things from upstairs. I'm just going to get changed—I won't be long.'

It took only a few minutes to straighten her desk and put the cover on her typewriter; then, picking up the script of *Valley of Destiny* ready to put it in a drawer, Jassy hesitated. From the start, the power of the script had caught her up in its imaginary world. Thinking as an actress, she had been able to visualise the scenes vividly, and the pages she had typed had only whetted her appetite to read more. No one would know if she took it home. She could read it overnight and return it the next day with no one any the wiser. Impulsively she slipped the folder into the roomy shoulder-bag that lay beside her desk.

The next task was to collect her few belongings from the bedroom, but once she had packed everything into her overnight bag Jassy found herself lingering inexplic-ably, recalling with painful clarity the thoughts and feelings that had assailed her in this room in the early hours of the morning.

Leigh might as well have made love to her, she reflected, because she would never be able to go back to the way she had been before. She had been smugly convinced of her ability to handle her sexual feelings, when the truth of the matter was that she had never felt anything approaching real sexual desire before. All her emotional energy had been directed towards her acting, the need to

prove herself to herself and to her parents uppermost in her mind so that she had never wanted
any more than the kisses and mild caresses she
had shared with her boyfriends.

But now, when a man she did not like, let alone
love, a man so cynical and arrogant that under
normal circumstances she would have avoided
him like the plague, could so easily make her
forget all her convictions, could bring her to the
point where she had desperately wanted him to
make love to her without any thought of the
consequences, she was forced to look at things in
a very different light. The shock of realising that
she was capable of experiencing such intense
physical passion had stripped away the self-
confidence she had built up over the years and
reduced her once more to the gauche, uncertain
girl she had been when she had first left home.
Deep inside, Jassy sensed intuitively that she
would never be able to respond to a man, any
man, in quite the same way again. After knowing
that sense of heightened awareness and need that
she had felt in Leigh's arms, would she ever again
be satisfied with the light-hearted lovemaking she
had enjoyed in the past?

Leigh was waiting for her when she went back
downstairs. He had discarded his casual shirt and
jeans in favour of a lightweight beige suit and a
bronze-coloured shirt that picked up the colour
of his eyes so that they reminded Jassy of the
watchful, golden gaze of a tiger. Seeing him, she
immediately wished she had insisted on catching
the bus. Dressed like this, Leigh was no longer

the man she had worked with all day, the polite if somewhat distant boss. With the change of clothes he had once more assumed the public image of Leigh Benedict, the film star, and the sheer force of his rugged sexual magnetism awoke memories of the previous night that almost overwhelmed her, making her feel shaky and ill at ease.

'Ready?' Leigh asked, glancing at his watch. He seemed impatient to be off, with no sign now of the reluctance he had appeared to feel earlier, so that Jassy was convinced that she must have misread his reaction.

Recalling the lascivious way Anna Golden had spoken of her plans to help Leigh unwind, her voice, her eyes, even her movements implying a sensual pleasure in simply anticipating the time they would spend together, she could not wonder at Leigh's impatience. No doubt the worldly actress would more than compensate him for the frustrations of the previous night, she told herself bitterly, and felt a slow, cold shiver slide down her spine at the thought of how she might have been feeling now if she had let Leigh make love to her, only to see him return to his mistress the very next day.

Leigh's car was as sleekly powerful as Jassy remembered it from the night of *Romeo and Juliet*, the sight of it reviving the feelings of anger and disgust she had felt then, so that she sat stiffly in her seat, holding her bag tightly in her lap, as Leigh swung the car out of the gate. She could only pray that the journey to her flat would not take long. The confined space of the car's interior had forced her into an intimate proximity to Leigh that was infinitely disturbing. She was shiveringly aware of the warmth of the lean body beside her, abnormally sensitive to the movements of his hands on the wheel as she stared fixedly ahead of her, unable to relax.

'What made you decide to take a secretarial course?' Leigh's quietly spoken question broke into Jassy's thoughts, so that she rushed into her answer without pausing to reflect whether she wanted to reveal anything so very personal to him.

'My parents hated the thought of my becoming an actress. They thought it was an unstable, insecure, and somehow very trivial sort of occupation. They wanted me to get a "real job", like my brothers and sister who are all highly respectable professional people. Acting, in their opinion, was better kept as an interesting hobby.'

She was unaware of the note of unhappiness that had crept into her voice at the recollection of her parents' opposition and scorn for her private dreams.

'It's certainly not a regular nine-to-five job,' Leigh put in drily. 'But, in my opinion at least, the rewards outweigh the disadvantages. I know that feeling of wanting—*needing*—to act, but I can also understand your parents' point of view. How did you get them to change their minds?'

'When I got a place at drama school, I was dependent on Mum and Dad for my living expenses—I only got a minimum grant. They still refused to let me go—until I came up with a compromise. I would do a secretarial course at an evening class, and then, if I couldn't get work as an actress, I would always have something to fall back on.'

'That sounds like an eminently sensible idea.' To Jassy's surprise there was a strong note of admiration in Leigh's quiet voice. 'There have been times when I've wished I had a second string to my bow; "resting" has to be the most inappropriate term ever. To an actor, it's more like living death.'

Jassy's attempt at laughter was shaken, uneven. She had never expected to find this degree of empathy between them.

'That's just how I feel. At times like this, I'm beginning to see what my parents meant.'

'You do keep in touch with your agent?' Leigh's tone was stern, very much the established professional advising a beginner in his field.

'Oh, yes, I ring her every day—but nothing's available. It's been three months now,' Jassy said on a sigh.

'Three months isn't so long. I was out of work for over a year at the beginning, and as I didn't have your practical forethought I ended up working behind a bar, hating every minute of it and convinced that I'd be there for the rest of my life. I was sure that my acting career was jinxed— finished before it had even begun.'

Jassy couldn't suppress a faint start of surprise. Success and acclaim seemed so intrinsically linked with Leigh's name that she found it hard to imagine him without them, as a beginner like herself, struggling to find a foothold on the rocky slopes of their profession. To her consternation, she found the image he had given her intensely appealing. It made him appear so very much more human than the godlike figure the newspapers and magazines had created.

'What broke the jinx?'

The question came a little breathlessly because something had made her heart kick painfully at the thought of Leigh at twenty or so, struggling to make his mark, younger, more innocent, without those cynical opinions that had so alienated her. Or had he always felt that way?

A brief grin flashed over Leigh's face, lighting it brilliantly for a moment.

'Would you believe pantomime?'

He glanced swiftly at Jassy's dumbfounded expression and the grin widened devastatingly.

'It's true,' he assured her. 'I played Wishee Washee in *Aladdin* in some ropey little provincial theatre. I sang, I danced, told appalling jokes— I even did a little magic.'

Jassy's heart jerked again, but this time it was not the past that had affected her but her instinctive response to that wide, unconstrained smile. This was a side to Leigh she had never seen before, and it was one she found herself liking very much. Encouraged by his more open, approachable mood, she found herself responding with enthusiasm.

'Funnily enough, it was a pantomime that got me hooked. I was seven years old and Mum and Dad took me to see *Cinderella*. It was the first time I'd ever been inside a theatre and from the moment the show started I knew that this was what I wanted to do. I pestered my parents to let me join a children's theatre club on Saturday mornings, and then, later, I joined the local amateur dramatic group.'

'Your parents didn't object to that?'

'Not when it was just a hobby. It was only when I wanted to make a *career* out of it that they objected. I knew that it would be very hard work, that if I made any sort of living out of acting I'd be incredibly lucky, but I never expected instant stardom.'

Would he let her get away with another question? She was going to risk it anyway; there was so much she wanted to ask him.

'When did you know that acting was what you wanted to do?'

'I don't remember ever making that decision. I spent so much of my early childhood in and around theatres that I thought that was the only way to exist. It was only later that I learned that not everyone lived that way, and then—people—tried to dissuade me.'

'Your parents?'

The words slipped out before Jassy had time to consider whether they were wise or not, and she knew immediately that they had been a mistake as Leigh's face changed dramatically, setting in hard, distant lines, the atmosphere in the car turning from springlike warmth to icy winter in an instant.

'My father was never around to comment,' Leigh said curtly. 'And as my mother had been dead for years by the time I decided on what I wanted to do, her opinion was irrelevant—though I doubt if she'd have encouraged me to follow in her footsteps.'

'Your mother was an actress?'

Curiosity overcame Jassy's repugnance at the darkly sardonic way Leigh had spoken of his parents. 'I spent so much of my early childhood in and around theatres,' he had said; that was something she hadn't known. There had been no mention of it in the brief biography that was used for publicity purposes.

'Who— ?'

'She didn't act under her real name,' Leigh snapped, clearly anticipating her question, and equally obviously not liking it. 'We're here.'

And if they hadn't arrived outside her flat at that point, Jassy thought, he wouldn't have answered any more questions—that much was evident from the tautness of every muscle in his face, the way his mouth was drawn into a thin, hard line. That part of Leigh's life was definitely not for public consumption, his expression said—and who could blame him? she acknowledged, considering privately how she would feel if the Press began poking around into her own family background.

As the car came to a halt Jassy hastily gathered her belongings together and got out, feeling suddenly supremely conscious of the contrast between the shabby, run-down street where she lived and Leigh's elegant town house.

'What time do you want me to come in tomorrow?' she asked jerkily, anxious for him to be gone and yet strangely reluctant to be the one who moved away first, the loss of that unexpected openness and sharing nagging at her like an aching bruise in her mind.

'After ten will do.' Leigh's response was abstracted, his thoughts seeming to be elsewhere—probably already on his evening with Anna Golden, Jassy told herself, and was shocked to find how much that fact stung.

The slight movement of a curtain at an upper window caught her eye and she groaned inwardly. Sarah must have heard the car and had come to see who had brought her home. Suddenly she became painfully aware of how foolish she must look, lingering in the rain when any sensible person would have hurried inside.

'I'll see you tomorrow——' she began, but Leigh had already started the engine. Without so much as a glance at her he steered the car away from the kerb and a few seconds later it had turned the corner and was out of sight.

Jassy had barely reached the top of the stairs before the door to the flat opened and Sarah appeared, fairly bubbling with excitement and curiosity.

'Was that who I think it was? What's been going on? Jassy, you've got to tell me *everything*!'

'There's nothing to tell.'

Wearily Jassy followed her friend into the flat, dropped her bags on the floor, and sank down into a chair. Leaning her head back against it, she rubbed her temples hard, trying to soothe the ache that had started as she had watched Leigh drive away.

'Nothing to tell?' Sarah echoed incredulously. 'That wasn't Steve's car, so it must have been the man himself. It *was* Leigh Benedict, wasn't it?'

'Yes, it was,' Jassy admitted tiredly. She didn't want to talk about Leigh, didn't want to *think* about him again tonight. Never before had any man raised such ambiguous feelings in her; she seemed to have been veering between attraction and repulsion with exhausting frequency all day long as if she were on some crazy emotional roller-coaster.

She glanced thoughtfully round the room, half expecting to find that it had changed in the time she had been away. She hardly felt like the same person as the girl who had left for work the morning before. But the flat was reassuringly same, though it looked shabbier than ever after the luxury of Leigh's home.

It had looked worse than this, she reflected, remembering the dark, drab little rooms before she and Sarah had put up posters, added cushions, but at least it was homely and she was fond of it. She frowned slightly at the memory of Leigh's indifference to his luxurious sur-roundings. From the things he had let sli~ his early struggle for success, she wo~ thought that he would take a great deli~

material wealth his fame had brought him—but then, on several occasions, Leigh had proved himself to be very different from what she had expected.

Becoming aware of Sarah's curious gaze, Jassy forced a smile.

'Sorry,' she said hastily. 'It's been a long day and Mr Benedict's not a man to let grass grow under his feet.'

She saw her friend's eyebrows lift at the formal 'Mr Benedict' and admitted to herself that she had used the words deliberately in an attempt to distance herself from the man who, in her private thoughts, she had thought of as Leigh all day.

'He works non-stop and expects everyone else to do the same. I've got to go in tomorrow too.'

'Is that all you're going to tell me?' Sarah put in plaintively. 'Why did he bring you——?'

'Sarah, it was raining. He gave me a lift home because he was coming this way anyway. He was going to see Anna—his...' she couldn't understand why she was having trouble getting the word out '...his mistress,' she finished baldly.

'Anna Golden? I didn't know she was still in favour. I thought he'd moved on to pastures new—and younger. But tell me, is he really as gorgeous as he seems on film? Oh, those eyes!'

Sarah rolled her own eyes and sighed dramatically, making Jassy laugh naturally for the first time.

'He's just as good-looking in the flesh, in fact more so, but——' Jassy sobered abruptly '—he ⟨kno⟩ws it. He's an arrogant devil—just because producers are down on their knees begging him to appear in their latest film, it doesn't give him the right to treat the rest of us mere mortals as less than the dirt beneath his feet!'

The uneasy awareness of the fact that she was speaking considerably less than the truth, the memory of Leigh's genuine concern and consideration for her—as his employee, at least—gave Jassy's words an unusual ferocity that Sarah noticed at once.

'He has put your back up, hasn't he? This can't be just because he didn't see your brilliant Juliet—I didn't either, and you haven't murdered me yet. What *did* he do?'

'He——' Jassy began and then stopped.

What *had* Leigh done? He had kissed her, had tried to make love to her, something other men had done without making her feel like this. Jassy could just imagine Sarah's reaction if she told her that.

Because, looking back, she was disturbed to find that she now saw the scene in Leigh's livingroom with very different eyes and, to her mental discomfort, she found it hard to condemn Leigh himself as totally as she had done then. *She* had behaved totally inexplicably, completely out of character, rational thought washed away on that crazy tide of need to touch Leigh, and, seen through his eyes, the situation could have had a very different interpretation.

What was it Leigh had said? He had responded as any normal man would when he'd found her practically in his lap, and for that she hated him?

Those other, detestable words, 'What is it you're after?' burned in her mind, but, strangely, she couldn't bring herself to speak them to Sarah, even though to do so would easily explain her antipathy towards Leigh Benedict.

'He——' she tried again, not really knowing what she was going to say, but at that moment the sound of the doorbell announcing the arrival of Sarah's boyfriend diverted her friend's attention.

Jamie's appearance turned the conversation on to more general topics, and a short time later he and Sarah departed for their night out, much to Jassy's relief. If her friend had persisted with the subject of Leigh Benedict, she had no idea how she would have answered. The man she hated was one side of him, but the man she had found so easy to talk to, both last night and again in the car, was a very different matter.

That particular quandary wasn't one she felt ready to cope with, so she made a determined effort to push it to the back of her mind as she prepared and ate a light meal then ran a warm, perfumed bath, feeling the tension in her neck and shoulders that had plagued her all day begin to ease as she relaxed lazily. A while later, dried and dressed in a light cotton robe, she gave in to the temptation that had been tormenting her all evening and allowed herself to open her bag and take out the script, curling up on the old, battered settee to read.

Time slipped away as she instantly became absorbed, the scenes coming vividly alive in her mind so that once or twice she spoke the heroine's words out loud, knowing instinctively how they should be delivered. Every page was evidence of the fine, intelligent mind she had seen at work earlier in the day, the part of Leigh that she could respect without constraint, ignoring other, less attractive aspects of his character. If he saw this film as a way of proving that intelligence to the world, then she could have no doubt that he would succeed.

All the time she was reading, a small, insistent voice at the back of Jassy's mind was saying over and over again, 'I *want* this part.' It was the part of a lifetime; the sort of role that any actress would give everything she possessed to be able to play, and she felt she was beginning to understand just why Leigh was having so much trouble casting it. Clara had to age over fifteen years in the course of the film, appearing first as a child of fourteen then maturing into a sophisticated woman, yet still retaining an essential innocence. There was no thought now of proving herself or winning acclaim in Jassy's mind—it was *Clara* she wanted to play.

But she had promised herself that she would never use her position to her own advantage, that she would never take anything at all from Leigh. That thought had her closing the script hurriedly, knowing that to continue reading it was just a masochistic form of self-torture when her private vow meant that, even if Leigh were to offer her a chance of auditioning for the role, she would have to refuse.

But there was no way she could leave Clara's story unfinished—and, anyway, there was no chance at all of Leigh offering her an audition. It was more likely that her eyes would turn green, knowing how he felt about her, she admitted with painful realism, a deep sigh escaping her as she opened the file again.

A short time later, deeply involved in a passionate scene between Clara and the male lead, Francis, Jassy imagined herself and Leigh speaking the words, trying to picture the intensity of the moment enhanced by the performance she knew Leigh to be capable of giving. The realisation of what she was doing brought her head up sharply and she found herself staring blankly at the wall, her mind whirling.

What was she thinking of? There wasn't the slightest chance of her ever being considered for the role of Clara, but even if there were, could she possibly act such a scene with *Leigh*? She had little doubt that he would be able to put aside any personal feelings and concentrate solely on the character he was playing, but could she? Would her training, the techniques she had learned so rigorously, be any defence against the feelings he could arouse in her simply by existing? She knew that Leigh had told her that he was concentrating on directing *Valley of Destiny*, but that was no comfort; it did nothing to ease the uneven thud of her heart that had started simply as a result of just *thinking* of those moments in Leigh's arms.

From the time Leigh had appeared in the kitchen of his home, the atmosphere between them had been highly charged, like the growing tension before a storm finally broke, as it had done last night. Never before had she felt so totally out of control. For the first time in her life she knew what it really meant to want a man physically, and she had been fool enough to pick on, as the object of that newly awakened desire, a man who felt nothing but contempt for her.

Sarah had a phrase for it, 'Falling into lust,' she called it, and the words came home to Jassy with a new and disturbing force because they described exactly how she felt about Leigh Benedict. But what made matters so much worse was the fact that if he should even suspect how she was feeling he would simply rank her with the women who were attracted to the sex-symbol image he so detested, or the actresses who would sell themselves to anyone with the influence that could be used to help them.

Jassy hated the idea of being thought of in that way, every ounce of self-respect she possessed cried out against it, but she didn't know how long she could continue to work for Leigh and manage to hold out against what she was feeling without giving herself away completely. She had the frightening feeling that she was sitting on a keg of gunpowder and someone had lighted a slow-burning fuse. She could only pray that the fuse was long enough to allow her to get through the rest of her time as Leigh's secretary before the gunpowder exploded right in her face, scarring her for life.

CHAPTER FOUR

THEY were all still at the breakfast table when the doorbell rang suddenly, shattering the lazy Sunday morning atmosphere.

'Who can that be?' Sarah asked, puzzled. 'No one we know is ever out and about before midday on a Sunday—and it's only just nine now.'

'Well, you'd better go and answer it,' Jamie said with a grin. 'You're the only one who's respectable.'

Glancing down at herself, and then at Jamie, Jassy had to agree that he was right. For some time now, Jamie had been a permanent fixture in the flat at weekends, and Jassy was well accustomed to his appearing at the breakfast table in his scruffy old dressing-gown. She liked Jamie—he and Sarah were clearly crazy about each other, and were saving hard to be able to turn their relationship into a permanent one—and she had fallen into the way of treating him like one of her brothers, keeping to her old habit of enjoying a lingering Sunday morning breakfast while still in her nightclothes. This particular morning, it was Sarah's turn to make the regular weekly trip to the launderette, so she was the only one fully dressed.

'They're getting impatient,' Jamie added as the doorbell rang again, more loudly this time.

'Who do you think it could be?' Jassy wondered aloud as Sarah left the kitchen.

'No idea.' Jamie was concentrating on spreading marmalade thickly on his toast.

'Perhaps it's Sarah's mother,' Jassy suggested wickedly, knowing how very much in awe of Mrs Templeton Jamie was.

Jamie's look of dismay was so comical that she couldn't help laughing at his discomfiture, and a few moments later Jamie joined in. They were both still chuckling when Sarah returned.

'A visitor for you, Jassy,' she announced.

'For me?'

The look on her friend's face should have warned her; Sarah's eyes were glowing with barely suppressed excitement. As Jassy glanced towards the door every trace of laughter faded from her own face as she recognised the tall, golden-haired figure that now appeared behind her flatmate.

Her first coherent thought was that Leigh was wearing the same clothes that he had had on the night before, when he had been on his way to visit Anna Golden. The logical conclusion to be drawn from that was that he had not been home at all, but had spent the night with Anna—which was exactly what Jassy would have expected, so she was stunned to find that the thought brought a sudden, stabbing pain that was thoroughly disconcerting. Why should she care where Leigh had spent the night—and with whom?

Suddenly she became embarrassingly aware of the way she was staring, gaping bemusedly at Leigh, who was obviously waiting for her to speak.

'Good morning,' she managed, her voice infuriatingly breathless and uneven, revealing too much of the disturbed state of her thoughts.

Leigh's only response was a slight inclination of his blond head in acknowledgement of her greeting. He too looked slightly less composed than she would have expected, almost as if it had been as much of a shock to find himself here as his arrival had been to her. Jassy wished he would say something, anything to break the silence that seemed to be stretching out her nerves to snapping point. Luckily, at that moment, Sarah took charge.

'Won't you sit down, Mr Benedict?' she said, pulling out a chair. 'Would you like some coffee?'

'I'd love some.' Leigh spoke at last, lowering himself into the chair and stretching his long legs out in front of him. 'And, please, not Mr Benedict—Leigh will do.'

Still struggling for composure, Jassy suddenly thought that she had never fully realised just how attractive Leigh's voice was; it was as if she were hearing it for the first time. In fact, seeing him here in her flat, away from his usual surroundings, she felt as if she were seeing him for the first time. Even sitting down, the tall, lithe body seemed to dominate the small room. The golden hair was almost too bright in the morning sunlight, the tawny eyes incredibly clear and mesmerising, and Leigh's immaculate appearance, the superb cut of his clothes were in stark contrast to Jamie's ancient dressing-gown and unshaven face.

The thought of Jamie, sitting silently beside her, jolted Jassy back to reality. 'I'm sorry,' she said hastily, 'I should have introduced you. Sarah's my flatmate—and this is Jamie.'

As Jassy's slight gesture drew Leigh's attention to the man at her side she was stunned by the swift change in the actor's face. She could not miss the way the bronze eyes narrowed sharply as they rested on Jamie then swung back to her own face, darkened by a look of such scathing contempt that it almost seemed to scorch her skin.

For a moment she was bewildered, unable to see any reason for Leigh's reaction, then it came home to her that Jamie's dishevelled appearance and the way she was dressed, wearing only a pink cotton nightshirt, could make it appear that they, and not Jamie and Sarah, had just got out of the same bed—which was obviously the conclusion Leigh had come to. Anger flared at the thought that he might actually believe she was capable of trying to seduce him when she was already sleeping with someone else, putting a defiant note in her voice when she spoke.

'Was there something you wanted, Mr Benedict?' she asked, meeting his eyes deliberately, refusing to let that direct tawny gaze disconcert her, and carefully emphasising the formal 'Mr Benedict' so that it was obvious she was ignoring his instructions to use the more familiar 'Leigh'.

'Yes—you,' Leigh answered softly, the tiniest flicker of a smile showing that he'd registered her involuntary start of surprise. 'I thought you might want a lift into work,' he continued evenly. 'So as I was coming this way I called in.'

It was all perfectly reasonable and considerate of him, Jassy told herself; he was being the perfect boss again. So why did she feel so hostile, prickling all over like a cat faced with an intruder into its territory? It couldn't be just because he had so obviously come here straight from Anna.

'But you said after ten!' she protested, voicing her only real grievance. 'I'm not ready!'

She regretted the words as she saw the way Leigh's eyes dropped from her face to survey her body in a swift, appraising glance that made her feel hot and then shiveringly cold as she became intensely aware of just how little she had on. All the mornings Jamie had been there, he had never once made her feel like this. Leigh's glance seemed to strip away the delicate pink cotton, revealing her nakedness beneath it.

Jassy shifted uneasily on her chair, trying to tuck her long, slender legs further under the table to hide them from Leigh's probing eyes. She was deeply grateful for the fact that Jamie and Sarah had started a conversation of their own and seemed oblivious of her embarrassment.

'I am rather early, I admit.' The blandness of Leigh's tone was almost shocking in contrast to the burning light in his eyes. 'But there's no rush. I can wait.'

He lounged back in his chair, reaching for his coffee, totally at his ease. Damn the man! Jassy thought angrily. This was her flat, yet he looked so completely at home, somehow managing to make *her* feel as if she were in alien territory.

'I'd better get dressed, then,' she declared tautly, getting to her feet.

'Don't hurry on my account,' was the silkily murmured response. 'I'm perfectly happy to wait.'

The warmly sensual light in his eyes, the way his gaze went deliberately to the length of her legs beneath the short nightshirt made Jassy's cheeks burn hotly, and she had to bite her tongue to keep back the angry retort that sprang to her lips.

What had brought about this sudden change in attitude? In contrast to the man who only the day before had made it painfully clear that he had no interest in her as a woman, it now seemed that he was openly flirting with her, encouraging the sort of attention he had repulsed so violently, and for the life of her she couldn't understand why.

'I wouldn't want to waste your time, Mr Benedict,' she said tartly, smiling slightly to herself as she saw that the double-edged comment was not lost on him. 'I realise that you must be anxious to get to work.'

Leigh smiled lazily over the top of his coffee-mug. 'Not at all,' he drawled, then, taking the ground from beneath her feet, added softly, 'Right now, work is the last thing on my mind.'

Her face bright scarlet, Jassy fled from the room. Once, just once, she would like to get the better of him, but somehow he was always one step ahead of her.

She had just finished dressing when a brisk tap at the door announced Sarah's arrival in search of Jassy's contribution to the washing bundle.

'You're not going like that!'

'Why not?' Jassy asked defensively, considering her reflection in the mirror. The navy skirt and yellow short-sleeved shirt might not be brand-new, but they looked perfectly respectable. 'I wore this outfit last week and you didn't make any comment then.'

'But there was only Steve there last week— Leigh's quite different. You ought to dress up a bit—impress him.'

'I don't want to impress him!' Jassy declared, reaching for a brush and pulling it through the long, pale curtain of her hair, avoiding her friend's eyes as she did so, afraid her discomposure would be only too clear in her face.

'Oh, come off it, Jassy! He's Leigh Benedict!'

'So? He's just a man—and *not* the sort of man *I* want to impress. I don't like him, Sarah.'

'I can't see why.' Sarah looked genuinely puzzled. 'I think he's a real charmer—and gorgeous with it. But, like him or not, wouldn't it do your career prospects some good if he were to notice you?'

It's likely to do just the opposite, Jassy was tempted to retort, but, conscious of the awkward questions that remark might lead to, she hastily bit the words back.

'You know that's not the way I want to do things, Sarah. If someone offers me a part, I want it to be because I can *act*, not because of who I know.'

'But surely it wouldn't hurt to be specially nice to him—just in case?'

'It would hurt my self-respect.' The knowledge of all she was holding back made Jassy's voice sharp. 'Besides, I couldn't use anyone in that way.'

'Well, it's up to you. If you want to miss out on the best chance of getting your foot in the door of the film world you're ever likely to get, that's your business—but I think you're crazy—especially when he seems to fancy you.'

'What?' Jassy's brush stilled abruptly and she stared at Sarah's reflection in the mirror, her own eyes wide grey pools of shock. 'What are you talking about, Sarah? Leigh doesn't *fancy* me!'

'I wouldn't be so sure about that,' Sarah declared archly. 'I saw the way he looked at you—and he didn't have to come and collect you this morning, did he?'

'No...'

Jassy allowed herself half a minute to consider the possibility that what Sarah had said might conceivably be true. How would she feel then? It would be flattering, to say the least, to know that a man who could have his pick of the most beautiful women available should even think her attractive. Jassy considered her own face in the mirror and was thoroughly disconcerted to see a new and unexpected glow in her soft grey eyes, a softness round her mouth, colour flaring high on her cheekbones. Then reason prevailed and, with an effort, she drove such fanciful thoughts from her mind.

'Don't be daft!' The words were addressed to herself as much as to Sarah. 'Why should he even look twice at me when there are women like Anna Golden around? And, as for coming to collect me—well, you heard the man. He was coming this way so he called in. If I know him, he's only here because he wants to make sure I get in a full day on that precious script of his.'

That comment reminded her that Leigh's 'precious script' was still on her bedside table. Picking up the folder, she pushed it deep inside her bag, zipping the bag up firmly as a protection against Leigh's probing eyes.

'All right, have it your own way!' Sarah sighed her exasperation. 'So he's not interested—but I still think you could get him to be.'

'No, thanks!' Jassy said swiftly. The brief experience she had had of Leigh being 'interested' had disturbed her enough already.

'Why not? Jassy, what is this with you and Leigh? I've never known you react like this before. What happened between you two?'

'I told you last night.'

'You told me nothing last night! All you gave me was a load of guff about his being arrogant and unpleasant—none of which fits with the man I've just been talking to.'

'We just didn't hit it off. It happens, Sarah.'

'But not with you—you're one of the most tolerant people I know, and you've never taken such an instant dislike to anyone.'

Jassy couldn't cope with any more. How could she answer Sarah's questions when she couldn't even answer her own?

'Leave it, will you, Sarah? I have to go. Leigh will be sick and tired of waiting.'

In fact, Leigh looked anything but impatient at being kept waiting. His jacket discarded and slung carelessly over the back of a chair, he was deep in conversation with Jamie, and Jassy's heart lurched treacherously as she registered once more how vital and attractive a man he was. It seemed impossible that any one man could have so much: looks, talent, money, and—yes, charm. Jassy had to admit that. Catching him unawares like this, seeing his hard face suddenly animated and smiling, she could see why Sarah found it so hard to understand her own dislike of him. And then, unwanted, her flatmate's other comment slid insidiously into her mind.

Could this devastating man really be attracted to her? At that moment Leigh glanced up, that smile still lingering on his face, making her heart jolt painfully in her chest so that she had to catch her breath before she could speak.

'I'm ready—I hope I didn't keep you waiting too long.'

'Not at all. I was just thinking that it's a pity we have to work at all today. I'd be quite happy to stay here all morning.'

Jassy couldn't think of the right way to react. She was not at all sure just what role Leigh was playing now; she only knew that it was not the remote, distant boss of the day before. Awkwardly she fumbled with her jacket, avoiding the 'I told you so' look she knew must be on Sarah's face. Leigh got to his feet, taking the jacket from her and holding it out for her.

'Thank you.'

Jassy's voice was very low, just a murmur, as she slid her arms into the sleeves, her heart seeming to beat high up in her throat in response to his closeness. As Leigh adjusted the jacket over her shoulders, gently freeing a long strand of fair hair that had caught under the collar, the tips of his fingers brushed the delicate skin of her neck in a brief, tantalising touch that was almost a caress, sending a *frisson* of reaction running down her spine. For a moment his hands seemed to linger on her shoulders as if he was reluctant to release her, but so fleetingly that Jassy couldn't be sure that she hadn't imagined it, because a second later he had moved away and was shrugging himself into his own jacket, thanking Sarah for the coffee as he did so.

'You must come again,' Sarah told him, blithely ignoring the furious glare Jassy shot at her. 'Perhaps you'd like to come round for a meal some time.'

'I'd like that.' Leigh's eyes slid to Jassy's face and she saw the challenging light in them. 'Will you be there or is there someone who might object?'

The look he slanted in Jamie's direction told Jassy all she needed to know. So no one had enlightened him about Jamie's true position! She didn't even try to hide the triumph in her eyes as she answered him.

'This is Sarah's flat as much as mine,' she told Leigh sweetly. 'She's entitled to invite anyone she likes for a meal, and if Jamie doesn't mind your visiting his girlfriend, then I can see no reason why anyone else might object.'

Her sense of triumph grew as she saw anger darken Leigh's eyes as he realised his mistake and the way she had turned it back on him. Intoxicated by the knowledge that at last she had got the better of him, Jassy could not resist adding, 'And I doubt if Steve would object if I joined you. He would understand that sometimes a secretary has to have dinner with her boss, even if it's more of a duty than a pleasure.'

And that was probably the best exit line she was going to get! Not even looking at Leigh to see how he had reacted to her final dart, she tossed her hair back in a defiant gesture and left the room, running lightly down the stairs without a backward glance.

Leigh caught up with her at the front door. Before she could slam it shut behind her, his hand closed over her wrist, strong fingers digging into her skin so that she winced with pain as he swung

her round to face him, his topaz eyes glittering
with cold anger.

'What the hell do you think you're playing at?'
he demanded in a low, furious voice and Jassy
flung up her head to meet his savage gaze.

'I'm not playing at anything, Mr Benedict,' she
declared, her own voice cold and tight. 'This is
no game, I can assure you; I meant what I said.
Now would you please let go of my wrist? You're
hurting me.'

'And have you try to run away again?' Leigh
shook his head adamantly. 'No chance. We have
some talking to do.'

'I have nothing to say to you,' Jassy declared,
turning her face away from him and staring determinedly out across the street. Leigh sighed his
exasperation.

'Well, I've got plenty to say to you, sweetheart. I'm not at all sure what's going through
that pretty head of yours, but I think it's time I
found out—so we talk. It's your choice—we can
have this conversation here or at my place.'

That brought Jassy's head swinging round to
him again.

'Are you suggesting that I'm ever going to set
foot in your house again?' she demanded furiously. 'Because if so, you'd better think again.
I don't want to go anywhere with you!'

'You have some work to do, remember?' Leigh
reminded her almost gently and, tormented by
thoughts that constantly swung from one ex-
treme to another without any sort of resolution,

Jassy felt she'd had more than enough of this situation and threw caution to the winds.

'I have no intention of working for you ever again!' she stormed, not caring that her voice sounded unnaturally loud in the quiet street. 'Get yourself another secretary—I'm leaving!'

'But I don't want another secretary.' Leigh's softly spoken words were shaded with a touch of menace that sent a shiver down Jassy's spine. 'You suit me fine; I have no complaints about your work. So why don't we get into the car and go back to the house so that we can talk this out like two rational adults? People are starting to notice us,' he added in an infuriatingly reasonable voice.

'I'm not going anywhere with you!'

Jassy felt as if she were banging her head against a wall; Leigh's immovable calm only seemed to aggravate the incoherence of her own whirling thoughts. How had she got herself into this situation? In desperation she fought to free herself from Leigh's restraining hand, but in vain. Her struggles merely drew the attention of an elderly couple who were passing and who frowned reprovingly at such a disturbance on a peaceful Sunday morning.

'See?' Leigh's amused voice sounded very close to Jassy's ear, his breath stirring her hair, brushing over her skin where her nerves were so hypersensitive to his nearness that the its soft touch seared through her, making her shudder in reaction. 'Why don't you stop making an exhibition of yourself?'

Jassy wanted to scream. Leigh clearly had no intention of releasing her unless she did as he said, but the thought of being alone with him—and her own unpredictable, inexplicable reactions—was more than she could bear.

'I don't give a damn if people stare!' she hissed at Leigh. 'I'm not the one with an image to keep up! Is that what's worrying you?' she demanded vindictively. 'Will it damage your bright public image to be seen like this? Leigh Benedict, superstar, idol of millions, caught with the one woman who can't stand the sight of him—it's not quite what the papers like to print, is it?'

She flung the words at Leigh's face, fully expecting to see the hard, set mask darken in anger, but, amazingly, Leigh smiled. Jassy didn't like that smile one little bit; it was slow, cynical, curling his lips, but never reaching his eyes, not lighting his face at all.

'On the contrary,' he told her silkily, 'that's just the sort of story the papers would love—and it's a story they'll get too if you don't see sense and get away from here before someone recognises me. I've told you, I don't give a damn about my image. The papers have printed what they like about me for years now, but it could make things difficult for *you*. So unless you want your face plastered all over the gossip columns tomorrow morning you'd better stop behaving like some three-year-old having a tantrum and get in the car.'

Still Jassy hesitated. She knew that what Leigh said was true, and was horrified at the thought of the disruption of her life that would follow any such publicity, but to obey Leigh was to admit defeat, something she was determined not to do. Leigh's grip on her arm tightened painfully.

'You have precisely ten seconds in which to make up your mind and come quietly,' he said in a low, dangerous voice. 'Because if you don't, I will pick you up and put you in the car myself—and to hell with the publicity if we're seen. I don't intend to wait around here all day—I have a script to work on and I've wasted enough time as it is.'

As Leigh's words reminded her of something that her anger had driven from her mind, the angry colour faded swiftly from Jassy's face, leaving her looking white and strained. A cold fear filled her mind and her fingers clenched tightly over the bulk of the script inside her shoulder-bag. She would have to go with Leigh now, if only to return the folder to her desk. Leigh's reaction if he discovered that it was missing was too terrifying to contemplate because she could imagine only too well just what interpretation he would put on that discovery. He would assume that her declaration of wanting nothing from him was a lie, that, when her seductive tactics had failed, she had taken the script to study in order to be able to impress him with her understanding of the part. No matter what she said, he would believe that she meant to use him for her own advantage.

'Your time's up.'

Jassy's shoulders slumped dejectedly. She felt suddenly exhausted; there was no fight left in her.

'I'll come,' she said dully.

If Leigh felt any surprise at her sudden surrender, no sign of it showed on his face as, with
his hand still on her arm, he steered her down the
steps and into the car, where she sat hunched in
her seat, staring gloomily out into the sunlit street.
As Leigh slid into his place beside her and leaned
forward to insert his key in the ignition, his arm
brushed against Jassy's in an unwelcome re-
minder of the way she had felt in this car the night
before, reawakening that overwhelming sense of
the nerves in her body coming tinglingly awake.
The sensation was intolerable in her present
mood, and without thinking she moved as far
away from him as possible, pressing up close
against the door in an effort to avoid any further
contact.

Out of the corner of her eye she saw the way
Leigh's hands tightened on the steering-wheel
until his knuckles showed white, and nerved
herself for the inevitable explosion. Surprisingly,
it didn't come; instead, Leigh's jaw clamped
tightly shut as if he was holding back some
furious response. His frightening silence lasted
the length of the time it took him to drive down
the street, then as they turned the corner he ex-
pelled his breath suddenly in a sigh.

'Just what is bugging you?' he demanded. 'I
can't make you out. I've only got to look at you
the wrong way and you explode. Just what is it
that makes you so hostile?'

'You!'

And me, she added more honestly in the privacy of her thoughts, because, deep down, she knew that her own behaviour was disturbing her far more than any of his. As Sarah had said, she wasn't usually the sort to take an instant dislike to anyone—and if dislike was all she felt, how much easier things would be.

'Me?'

Those tawny eyes swung round to her face, and for a moment Jassy almost believed that the perplexity in them was genuine—until she remembered just how well he could act.

'You don't like it, do you?' Something worryingly like disappointment made her voice coldly spiteful. 'You really can't believe that I might not like you. You claim you don't like your sexsymbol image, but you're so used to having every woman fall at your feet just because you're Leigh Benedict that you can't accept that there might be one woman who isn't susceptible to your looks and your money. Well, for your information, there is such a woman—me!'

In the silence that followed her outburst, the car careered around a corner with a violence that jolted Jassy roughly in her seat. Glancing hastily at Leigh, she shivered involuntarily as she saw the way his mouth was tightly compressed, his lips just a thin, hard line. For a few minutes more he drove the car in silence, manoeuvring the powerful vehicle at a speed that was positively dangerous, even in the comparative quiet of the Sunday morning traffic. Then, just as Jassy was beginning to feel distinctly panicky, he slowed gradually.

'No,' he said at last. 'That's not it. There's more to it than that.'

'Isn't that enough?' Jassy retorted, but some of the sting had gone from her voice. It had started out as mere dislike, but somewhere along the line it had got much, much more complicated.

'No,' Leigh said again. 'I don't think it is enough. If you're going to treat me as if I'm some appalling monster that's just crawled out of the primeval slime, then I reckon you owe me a bit more than, "I don't like you."'

On the last words his voice took on almost exactly the same intonation as Jassy's, so that she could not suppress an involuntary gasp of admiration—but one that was mixed with shame and embarrassment at hearing just how childish and petty her words had sounded.

'If you'll just let me explain...' she began hesitantly.

'I'm listening,' Leigh said quietly.

His stern, unrelenting profile offered no encouragement, but this might be the only chance she would ever get to convince him that, in her case at least, his cynical opinion of women was totally unjustified. Jassy didn't know why it was so very important, over and above the need to let him know she was not just a 'seductive little siren', she only knew that, at this moment, it mattered intensely to her that somehow they might just have come to some sort of turning-point, and that thought made her swallow hard before she spoke.

'I don't know why you have such a low opinion of women—and actresses in particular—but I object to being tried and condemned by you without any evidence or a chance to speak in my own defence. For your information, I have never offered any sort of "favours" to *anyone* to win any part, and I have no intention of ever doing so. I told my parents I was serious about acting, that if I had any talent I'd succeed, and I meant it. If I'm any good I'll succeed, but my *acting* is what matters. There's no satisfaction in winning any other way. Perhaps there are people who wouldn't think twice about jumping into bed with someone to further their career, but that's not the way I want to do it. It would destroy my self-respect.'

She paused, waiting for Leigh's reaction, but he kept his eyes on the road, no flicker of emotion crossing his face.

'Go on,' he commanded after a moment, and to Jassy's intense relief his voice seemed to have lost some of the acidic bite of moments before.

The next bit was more difficult.

'You seem to have assumed that just because you're Leigh Benedict and I'm female, the rest is automatic. When we first met you forced yourself—your kisses on me when it must have been clear that your attentions were repellent to me, and on Friday—— '

'On Friday?' Leigh echoed dangerously.

'You know what happened then! You took advantage of the fact that I was alone with you and tried to seduce me. I realise now that you must have thought I only took this job because I'd be working for the Golden Thief, but you couldn't be more wrong——'

Leigh's laugh broke in on her, a harsh, cynical sound that seemed to splinter the air inside the car.

'*I* tried to seduce *you*?' he declared sardonically. 'Well, that's an interesting twist, I must say. Let's get one thing straight, lady—you were the one doing the seducing. You were practically begging me to take you.'

Something seemed to explode inside Jassy's mind as Leigh's cold voice echoed over and over in her head. The fact that she couldn't deny her own part in Friday's events was swept away under a wave of fury, as was the memory of the other Leigh, the one she had actually found herself liking. All she could see was this arrogant devil of a man who was determined to think the worst of her. Her temper flared and, heedless of her own safety, she lashed out, striking Leigh hard on the temple with her clenched fist, jarring his head to one side.

For a moment the car veered dangerously across the road, narrowly avoiding crashing into a van parked on the opposite side, but Leigh's reactions were incredibly swift. His left hand shot out to push Jassy firmly back in her seat and hold her there while he controlled the car with the other. Seconds later, they had turned into a quiet side-street where he pulled up and sat silently for a moment, gripping the steering-wheel tightly as if he could not trust himself if he let go. The rigidly controlled violence in him terrified Jassy, so that she shrank back in her seat as Leigh rounded on her, his golden eyes blazing.

'Now *you'll* listen to me,' he told her in that low, dangerous voice Jassy had come to dread, his hands gripping her shoulders as if he wanted to shake her hard. 'You've been flinging accusations at me—now it's my turn, and you're going to listen if we have to stay here all day.'

Jassy knew she had no choice. The strength of Leigh's grip on her shoulders brought home to her forcefully just how little chance she had of getting away from him if she tried to struggle.

'All right,' she said flatly, 'I'm listening.'

Leigh released her immediately, his hands moving once more to the steering-wheel, his long fingers tapping restlessly on it, then stilling suddenly as he began to speak.

'Let me tell you a story.' The darkly sardonic tone was back, colouring his beautiful voice in a way that made Jassy's breath catch in her throat. 'It's about a young actress, a girl who'd just left drama college—the same one that you went to, as a matter of fact.'

Gemma Morgan. Jassy stiffened in her seat, remembering the exchange between Leigh and Benjy.

'I met her at a party given by one of her tutors. She seemed a nice enough kid, and I quite enjoyed talking to her, but that was all—on my part, at least. It wasn't enough for her, however. She spun me some tale about her car being out of commission and not being able to afford a taxi fare home, so, naturally, I offered her a lift. We'd barely got halfway down the street before she threw herself at me, blouse unbuttoned down to her navel, and her skirt somewhere around her waist—and, just in case I couldn't take a hint, she was extremely explicit as to what she wanted me to do.'

Leigh's mouth twisted bitterly at the memory and Jassy wasn't surprised. If the positions had been reversed, any woman would have been screaming accusations of assault, or at the very least sexual harassment, under those circumstances.

'I declined the offer,' Leigh continued laconically, 'and thought that was that—I couldn't have been more wrong. For the next few weeks I couldn't go anywhere without that young lady——' his intonation gave the word a meaning that was the exact opposite of its real one '—appearing in what she considered to be provocative and enticing outfits and trying to get me into bed with her. She even managed to persuade my housekeeper to let her into the house, and when I got home I found her waiting for me in my bed—stark naked. And all this was because she wanted to play the female lead in my latest film—and she was prepared to do anything to get the part. When she realised she was getting nowhere with me, she turned her attention to the director, using the same tactics.'

Jassy flinched inside at the searing contempt in Leigh's tone. It was no wonder he had been anxious to avoid meeting another one of Benjy's protégées after his experiences with Gemma.

'And she wasn't the only one—just the latest in a long line of young hopefuls who'd try any trick in the book to get what they want.'

There was a sour taste in Jassy's mouth, and a sense of nausea had invaded her as she listened to this sordid story. If Leigh had often been subjected to this sort of harassment then it was no wonder that he should feel so contemptuous of the Gemma Morgan type, especially if, according to what he had just told her, and much to her surprise, he had not, as many others would have done in his place, simply taken advantage of what was being offered without giving anything in return.

But all actresses weren't like that—the majority of them felt as she did, she was sure. She might understand Leigh's cynicism better now, but she still deeply resented the way he had lumped her in with Gemma Morgan without any concrete evidence—well, on only the flimsiest of evidence, she forced herself to amend with uncomfortable honesty.

'That still——' she began, but a flash of anger in Leigh's eyes silenced her. Suddenly she felt intuitively that there was more behind Leigh's attitude than he was admitting, but she didn't dare ask him anything further. She was still too frighteningly aware of his physical strength to risk adding fuel to the burning anger that seemed to have died down to a smouldering ember, recognisable only in the hard light in Leigh's eyes, the tautness of the muscles in his jaw.

'Now we come to Friday, when, as you so quaintly put it, I forced myself on you——'

'Why?' Jassy broke in, unable to stop herself.

'Why?' Leigh repeated the word as if he didn't quite understand it. 'Why did I kiss you?'

With a sudden, violent movement that made her start in panic he hit the steering-wheel hard with the edge of his hand.

'Dammit, woman, because I wanted to! I told you at the time—you're damnably attractive when you're angry. I kissed you because I wanted to more than anything else—as I want to kiss you now,' he added with disconcerting softness.

Shock made Jassy's eyes very wide and dark. Her throat was painfully dry and she swallowed hard to relieve it as Leigh reached out a hand to touch her cheek. Although the brush of his fingertips was as light as a butterfly's wing she couldn't stop herself from flinching away, her heart sinking as she saw the way his face hardened at her reaction, and he snatched his hand back swiftly as if he had been burned.

'But I won't,' he said in a flat, emotionless voice. 'Because you find my kisses repellent—or so you say.'

The momentary pause had brought about a dramatic change of mood. Those tiger's eyes seemed to burn into Jassy's grey ones, challenging and mesmerising all at once so that Jassy found herself unable to drag her gaze away.

'But don't kid yourself, sweetheart. I didn't imagine your response that first time—or again on Friday. You wanted what I was offering, wanted it every bit as much as I did—if not more. You were the one who did the seducing that night. What did you expect me to do when I woke up and found you draped across me—tell you a bedtime story? Tell me——' he demanded, his voice hardening sharply '—did you really panic, or did you plan to lead me on and then leave me cold like that?'

The taunting words showed painfully clearly that he hadn't believed a word Jassy had said. She had thought she might clear the air, but instead she was still torn between anger and an inexplicable, deep, aching hurt at the realisation that he still put her in the same category as Gemma Morgan and her type. And the real trouble was that, in all honesty, she could not deny that, if she had been in Leigh's place, that was how she would have interpreted her own actions too—but admitting that was far too dangerous.

'Stop it!' she cried desperately, her mind seeming to split in two. 'Why can't you leave me alone? I hate you!'

She wanted to believe that was true, but couldn't any longer. The truth was she didn't know what she felt.

'Do you?' Leigh enquired, unmoved. 'Or do you just hate me for saying what you don't want to hear? Why don't you face up to the truth? I don't mind admitting I want to make love to you—I'd be a fool if I didn't, you're a very lovely girl. But it's more than that—you're something special. I knew it from the moment I first saw you, even in that appalling matronly suit, with your hair scraped back into that unflattering bun. I knew then that I wanted you—I still do.'

Leigh's eyes were very deep and dark as he spoke, and Jassy felt as if she could lose herself completely in them. She couldn't believe what she had heard, and yet Leigh's words repeated over and over in her head. Such a short time before, she had flirted with the idea that this disturbingly attractive man might actually be interested in her, not really considering the matter seriously. Now he had declared quite openly that he thought her not only attractive but very desirable—and she was quite unable to cope with such a declaration, taken unawares by the warm glow that flooded through her at his words. She felt strangely breathless as if his words had struck her like a physical blow, and her blood was pounding in her veins, making her temples throb so that she felt giddy and filled with a strange, nervous desire to laugh. But there was no laughter in Leigh's face; he was deadly serious. Never before had Jassy felt so helpless, so very vulnerable.

'I—don't want you,' she managed with difficulty, the words sounding hopelessly unconvincing, even to her own ears.

'No?' Leigh questioned softly. 'Forgive me for doubting you, but I think that right now I'm a better judge of what you do want than you are yourself. Try admitting it,' he encouraged gently.

'We could have something very good, if only you'd stop fighting me.'

But Jassy was incapable of forming any coherent thoughts, let alone voicing them, as Leigh's arm slid around her shoulders, drawing her slowly towards him. As if in a dream she felt the warmth of his mouth on her forehead, her closed eyelids, and then, heartbreakingly briefly, on her lips.

'See?' Leigh whispered against her hair. 'There's nothing to be afraid of.'

Slowly he drew away from her again. Jassy's eyes felt heavy, as if she had just woken from a very deep sleep, and when she opened them Leigh's face was blurred, as if her eyes would not focus on him properly. When her vision cleared it was as if she were looking at some other man who was Leigh and yet somehow very different, and she knew that the change was not in him but in her mind, in the way she saw him. The long, silent moment was broken at last when Leigh moved to start the car again.

'I think we'd better get going,' he said quietly.

As he turned his head to check the street before pulling out he winced slightly as the movement jarred his bruised temple. Acting purely instinctively, Jassy reached out to touch the place where her fist had struck him, shame flooding through her at the thought of her own mindless violence as she felt the slight swelling just over the bone. What was it about this man that made her behave in such totally uncharacteristic ways?

'I'm sorry,' she said, her voice very low. 'I didn't mean to hurt you.'

'Yes, you did,' Leigh told her drily. 'But maybe I asked for it.'

With gentle fingers Jassy traced the shape of the bruise and heard Leigh's sharply indrawn breath.

'Does it hurt if I touch it?'

'A bit—but I reckon I can stand it. It's not the pain that's bothering me,' he added with a look that was so blatantly sensual and inviting that Jassy snatched her hand away again in a flurry of confusion.

Leigh laughed, this time in genuine amusement.

'As I said, I think we'd better get going. I don't think I could be answerable for the consequences if we stayed here.'

CHAPTER FIVE

IT WAS not until she saw the familiar bright red sports car parked in the courtyard that Jassy remembered that Steve was due back that morning, the realisation sending her thoughts into completely new channels. She had been grateful for Leigh's silence during what remained of the journey, needing a breathing-space, both mentally and physically, to absorb the new and bewildering developments and consider her own feelings about them. Suddenly the Jassy who had applied for the job as Leigh's secretary seemed like someone she had known a long time ago, almost a stranger, with none of the thoughts and feelings she was now experiencing.

Only hours before, she had been convinced that she actively disliked Leigh, had declared to his face that she hated him. Now she longed for the clarity of that emotion, but knew that the peace of such clear-cut feelings had gone for good. She only knew that with Leigh she felt fully alive as never before, seeing everything in a completely new way as if every sense had been heightened by his presence; yet at the same time she felt very much afraid. The nearest she had come to anything like this before had been in the moments standing in the wings, waiting for the cue for her first appearance, with a new performance ahead of her. In the short time it took to reach Leigh's house she had swung from exhilarating joy to overwhelming despair and back again with frightening rapidity, and finally got out of the car with nothing resolved.

It was strange, Jassy thought as she walked towards the house, how only the day before she had clung to the thought of Steve's return as a welcome protection from being alone with Leigh, but now she vaguely resented the fact that he would be there. She felt she needed more time to explore the change in her relationship with Leigh, to consider just what it meant for her future, because she had no doubt that her immediate future at least was intimately entwined with Leigh's. There was no going back, and, whatever happened, nothing would ever be the same again.

Steve was in the kitchen, the inevitable mug of coffee in his hand, and he waved it cheerfully at Leigh and Jassy as they came in.

'You timed that just right. Want some?'

'Just what I need,' Leigh said, pulling off his jacket and slinging it carelessly over a chair. 'Then I must have a shower and change before I start work.'

'You are a trifle overdressed for a day in the office,' commented Steve. 'I suspect you've only just got in from a night on the tiles.'

'Guilty, milord.' Leigh accepted his coffee with a grateful smile. 'I spent the night at Anna's—

and you needn't look so disapproving. I'm a big boy now; I can take care of myself.'

'Hmm.' Steve looked unconvinced. 'I still think——'

'Lay off it, Steve,' Leigh said abruptly, but without anger, as if this was an argument they had had many times before. 'We agreed to differ over Anna, so less of the big-brother act.'

'Have it your own way.' Steve was handing the second mug of coffee to Jassy. 'But I see she's been up to her old tricks again.'

He indicated the bruise on Leigh's face which had now darkened to a dull red, and Jassy tensed, waiting for his friend's reply.

'Oh, that.' Leigh touched the mark carelessly. 'No, that was my own fault—I—walked right into something.'

Jassy's initial rush of relief was swiftly replaced by another, far less comfortable concern. She had been fool enough to forget about Anna Golden. How could Leigh tell her that he wanted her, only an hour or two after he had left the actress's flat after having spent the night there?

But then, yesterday, Leigh had hesitated perceptibly before he'd spoken to Anna on the phone, and Steve had assumed that it had been the older woman who had bruised Leigh's face during a quarrel, his tone implying that such behaviour was commonplace, so perhaps the relationship between Anna and Leigh was not the thriving affair Anna had led her to believe. Jassy was stunned by the immediate lifting of her spirits at the thought.

'Sit down, Jassy.' It was Leigh who spoke. 'Enjoy your coffee. I know we have plenty to do, but I'm not such a slave-driver that I expect you to launch into it straight away.'

There was a new note of warmth in his voice, one so unmistakable that Jassy wondered if Steve noticed it too and what he made of it. But then Steve had never seen the two of them together before. He knew nothing about Friday night—was it really only two days ago? Jassy felt as if the events of that night were so firmly etched on to her brain that it seemed impossible that they had not sent reverberations out into the atmosphere, affecting even those who had not been involved.

'Did you get that damn script finished?' Steve asked, and Leigh nodded his response.

'Jassy started the typing yesterday, that's why I asked her to come in this morning. What about the house? Is it what we're looking for?'

'Perfect! And there was no trouble getting permission to use it—it's all signed and sealed.'

'Thank heaven for that! At least something's going right. Now, if we can just have some better luck with these wretched auditions we might actually be able to start work.'

Leigh was prowling restlessly about the room, his actions making Jassy think of the pacing of a caged tiger, reminding her irresistibly of that intangible, dangerous streak in his character, a controlled power that set him apart from all the other men she knew.

'For heaven's sake, man, ease up!' Steve protested. 'You only finished filming on Friday; can't you give yourself a day off once in a while? Jassy and I are only human, even if you're not—and, quite frankly, I could do with a break.'

'Soon—maybe—when we've found our Clara—but today I'll want details of that house. I'll have to see it myself as soon as possible.'

'OK, boss,' Steve sighed good-humouredly. 'I suppose I'd better get down to it.'

He drained the last of his coffee and went to put his mug in the sink, moving close to Leigh as he did so, and, watching them, Jassy was stunned by her own response. No one could ever have denied that Steve was a good-looking man—she had been very attracted to him herself, the first time they had met—and yet now it seemed that his appeal was completely overshadowed by the vibrant power of the man at his side, a power she had once foolishly dismissed as too showy.

If only she could have stayed attracted to Steve, how much easier things would have been. With Steve there would never have been the fear that her feelings might be misinterpreted, no memory of those past, cynical words to sour the present. But it wasn't Steve who had turned her world upside-down—it was Leigh.

Absorbed in her thoughts, Jassy was only vaguely aware of Steve's leaving the room. As she heard the door close behind him Leigh came to stand opposite her, on the other side of the table, his fingertips resting lightly on the polished surface.

'Don't look so worried, Jassy,' he said softly, clearly misinterpreting the reasons for her disturbed frown. 'Is it such a dreadful thing to know that I want to make love to you?' he added with gentle derision.

Jassy wished she could say yes, that that was the last thing she wanted, so would he please leave her alone, but she knew that would not be the truth. She was only just beginning to realise how much it *could* mean to her, how much she wanted Leigh to desire her in this way. The fuse on the powder keg was burning faster than she had ever expected, her memory of the man she had seen outside the college, the man who had so angered and alienated her, growing cloudy and dim, and as it faded so did her instincts for self-preservation. The fury and disgust she had felt then were not enough to overcome the new feelings she did not yet know how to handle.

'No,' she managed, her voice little more than a whisper. 'I'm flattered——'

'Flattered?' Leigh's laugh was harsh. 'I'd hoped for something more than that!'

Suddenly his expression changed, his eyes darkening as he reached out a hand to touch her hair, twining a pale, silky strand around his finger.

'But don't worry; it will come. I can wait. When I make love to you it will be because you want it every bit as much as I do—and you will. You do now, only you're too scared to admit it. But one day you won't be afraid any more, and

I'll be waiting. I reckon you'll be well worth waiting for.'

Jassy kept her eyes fixed on the table-top, unable to meet that searching tawny gaze. Even the light touch of Leigh's hand on her hair had her whole body crying out for more, and she was afraid that he would read her feelings in her eyes if she looked at him.

'One other thing,' Leigh went on, his voice hardening abruptly. 'Whatever there is between you and Steve will have to be sorted out. I don't share my women; even with my best friend.'

'There's nothing to sort out.'

The words slipped out before Jassy quite realised she had spoken. Looking back, she couldn't say whether she had exaggerated her friendship with Steve as a defence against Leigh's attentions or her own disturbing feelings, but either way it hadn't worked.

And what about you and Anna? Isn't that something that needs 'sorting out', she wanted to ask, but didn't dare. Behind her, the kitchen clock struck the half hour, and she grasped thankfully at the chance of escape offered by more practical concerns.

'I'll get started on that typing now,' she said hastily, getting to her feet in a rush that betrayed more of her inner feelings than any words could ever do.

As she moved past him Leigh caught her shoulders and swung her round to face him. From the look in his eyes she guessed at his intention and her heart lurched painfully. Not yet! She wasn't ready for things to move on a stage just yet!

Leigh's kiss was brief, warm, and sweet, and with a supreme effort Jassy managed to remain passive in his arms, neither responding to nor fighting against his embrace. Then he released her and turned her towards the door.

'Off you go,' he said lightly. 'If I can't have the lover just yet, I suppose I'll have to make do with the secretary.'

The trouble was, Jassy thought as she crossed the hall, that she was no longer sure which role she was playing any more—the secretary or the lover—she didn't even know which one she *wanted* to play.

Steve was in her office, looking flushed and rather annoyed, his hair slightly ruffled as if he had been pushing at it impatiently. Several drawers had been pulled out of her desk, and he was searching through one of them as Jassy opened the door.

'Just the person I need!' he exclaimed. 'Jassy, love, where have you put that damned script? Leigh said you had it yesterday, but I can't find the wretched thing anywhere.'

Jassy froze, her fingers tightening on her bag. 'The script?' she asked rather breathlessly, though she knew only too well what he meant.

'*The* script. The one and only final, revised version in existence—and worth several times its own weight in Oscars—hopefully. Where have you hidden it?'

The smile that accompanied his words calmed Jassy's racing heart. This was Steve she was dealing with, not Leigh.

'Don't panic,' she told him laughingly. 'I've got it here.' Unzipping her shoulder-bag, she pulled out the folder. 'It's quite safe. I took it home with me last night.'

'You did *what*?'

The steely voice exploded from the doorway behind her, coming with the force of a physical blow on Jassy's back so that she took an involuntary step forward before whirling round to face Leigh, quailing inside at the sight of the black fury that darkened his face.

'You did what?' Leigh repeated with icy menace.

'I took it home with me!' Jassy blurted the words out desperately. 'It's so much easier to type something if you know what's coming so I—I took it home,' she finished lamely, bitterly conscious of the half-truths she was telling, and the interpretation Leigh must inevitably put on her actions.

'You took it home.' Leigh repeated her words with cynical disbelief. 'You took it home to read— to make sure you could type it up correctly. Do you really expect me to believe that? Of course you had no other motive whatsoever.'

'Leigh, don't be ridiculous!'

'No!' Jassy and Steve spoke together. 'No! No! No!' Jassy went on despairingly as, looking into Leigh's eyes, she saw how the warmth and desire of only minutes before had vanished, leaving his face a mask of coldly savage anger, pain stabbing deep into her heart at the knowledge of what he must be thinking.

She had anticipated just such a reaction if Leigh had ever discovered that the script was missing, but that made it no easier to bear now—in fact, recent developments made the situation far, far worse. It seemed a bitterly ironic twist of fate that she and Leigh should have reached, if not a peace, then at least a sort of truce such a short time before, only to return to open hostilities almost immediately.

'It wasn't anything like that!' she declared vehemently. 'I wouldn't do that—I couldn't!'

Jassy almost choked on the words. She felt bruised and sore, hurting physically from the accusation blazing in Leigh's eyes.

An uncomfortable silence descended on the room as Leigh regarded Jassy's pale face and over-bright eyes, his tawny gaze coldly hostile. For one dreadful moment Jassy wondered if he could see into her mind, read her whirling thoughts, and know that she was not telling the whole truth. Because it wasn't the truth. Deep inside, she knew how much she desperately wanted to play Clara, but knew that that could never happen. Even if by some miracle that chance were to come her way, she would have to deny it to herself because of what had happened between herself and Leigh.

'For goodness sake, Leigh!' Steve exclaimed reproachfully. 'She's telling the truth—surely you can see that?'

Still Leigh was silent, every taut muscle in his body revealing the ruthless control with which he was holding his temper in check. The terrifying silence seemed to drag on endlessly, and in that time Jassy saw Leigh with a sudden sharp clarity as never before. She saw his face, bleak, hard and implacable, the golden chips of ice that were his eyes, and had to bite back the cry of pain that almost escaped her, feeling as if a knife were being slowly twisted in her heart. In that moment she felt as if she had lost something infinitely valuable, something as essential to her life as the air she breathed.

At last Leigh moved, shrugging indifferently.

'Maybe,' he said slowly, addressing his words to Steve, but then his eyes swung back to Jassy's face. 'But I'm warning you, one more trick like that . . .'

He left the rest of the sentence unspoken, but there was no need for him to say any more, and, as he turned on his heel and strode out of the room, the door slamming shut behind him, Jassy found that her legs would no longer support her and sank into a chair with a tiny, shocked gasp. Steve stared after Leigh, a stunned expression on his face.

'What the hell got into him?'

Jassy shook her head helplessly. 'Forget it, Steve,' she said in a low, shaken voice. 'You don't understand.'

Steve could never understand, not fully, because he had no idea of all that had passed between her and Leigh. There was no way he could

know that Leigh had reacted as he had because
less than an hour before he had admitted that he
was not objective where she was concerned.
Would she be a fool to hope that Leigh had turned
on her in this way because, after all, he *had* believed her when she had told him that she wanted
to succeed by her ability alone?

But then the truth hit home with the realisation
that, even if he had come anywhere near believing her, that tiny link between them had now
been broken and, once again, Leigh believed only
the very worst of her motives.

'You're damn right, I don't understand!' Steve
said grimly. 'But Leigh's not going to get away
with this.'

He was moving towards the door as he spoke
and, as she watched him, a cold panic filled
Jassy's mind. The mood Leigh was in, he would
probably believe that *she* had persuaded Steve to
talk to him.

'No, Steve—please——'

But she was too late; Steve had gone.

Left alone, Jassy sat as if frozen in her chair.
Only her hands moved, twisting tightly together
in her lap, but her mind was racing. Even the
memory of Leigh's anger had faded to a dull blur,
all but driven from her thoughts by the recollection of the moment when she had looked into
Leigh's hard, set face and felt that terrible sense
of loss. In that moment she had found herself a
prey to a host of totally new feelings.

Or, rather, not new, because now that she was
calm enough to think Jassy had to admit that

those feelings had been there from the moment Leigh had arrived back from Scotland, when she had seen him as if for the first time, but she hadn't recognised them for what they were. If she had, she would have fled from him then, abandoning her job, everything, mindful only of the foolishness of getting involved with a man as dangerous to her peace of mind as Leigh Benedict.

Because she *was* involved, there was no way she could deny that. With a sigh, Jassy acknowledged what she had been trying to hide from herself since the moment Leigh had first kissed her. It was as if in some strange way the whole of her life had been leading up to that moment, but she had tried to deny her instincts, had blurred the issue by dwelling on his arrogant behaviour, deceiving herself into believing that she positively disliked him. She couldn't have been more wrong.

Like or dislike didn't come into it; she *wanted* this man. He made her come alive, so fully alive that she wondered if she had been blind, deaf and dumb before now. He had only to touch her for her to know that she was truly a woman, with all the hopes, dreams and passions that had been buried for so long—buried under her ambition, her need to prove herself.

For the first time Jassy recognised that underneath her reluctance to commit herself to anything deeper than friendship with other men lay a fear, unacknowledged until now, that such commitment would drain the energy and dedication she devoted to her acting. With Leigh she hadn't even thought of that. It seemed that he possessed the key to the Pandora's box of feeling and desire that lay inside her, and he had used it to devastating effect. He wasn't right for her in the way she had dreamed of finding a man who would love her for the rest of her life, but she had fed too long on dreams. There would be no forever with Leigh; if she wanted him, she had to take the man he was.

But, after what had just happened, would Leigh ever let her near him again? He was even more convinced than before that all that attracted her to him was, as he had suspected all along, the power and influence he possessed, the public image of the Golden Thief. Jassy flinched away from the irony of the fact that, just as her behaviour seemed to have proved that fact, *she* had realised that the change in her feelings towards Leigh had come about when he had appeared in the kitchen wet and dishevelled, and, even more so, when he had seemed so boyishly vulnerable in sleep. In his own home he had cast aside the image he so hated and appeared as just a man; and it was *that* man whom Jassy wanted.

Upstairs a door banged shut and Jassy heard the sound of footsteps descending the stairs. Hastily she pulled her typewriter towards her, snatched off the cover and inserted a sheet of paper into the machine. Steve was coming back, and she didn't want him to find her sitting here like this. If he did, he would inevitably ask questions—questions she wouldn't know how to answer.

Acting purely automatically, Jassy adjusted the paper in the typewriter and opened the folder that contained the film script. She even managed to type a line or two before the door opened, and did not look up as quiet footsteps crossed the room and a tall figure came between her and the light from the window, throwing a long shadow over the page.

'Steve informs me that I'm a heartless swine,' a quiet, ruthlessly controlled voice said. 'In fact, from what he told me, I'm surprised to find you're still here. He had me convinced that you would be unable to tolerate my hateful presence any longer.'

Jassy's fingers froze over the typewriter keys and she kept her eyes fixed on the sheet of paper in front of her until the words on it blurred into each other. She should have known it was Leigh! Some sixth sense should have warned her as soon as he opened the door.

That stiffly polite voice seemed to drain all the warmth from her blood as she listened to it. Was this the same man who had kissed her with such passion just two days before, and again, with gentle tenderness, only that morning? There was no trace of passion in his tone now, and as for tenderness—such an emotion seemed totally alien to the man before her. Keeping her head lowered, Jassy said nothing and waited for Leigh to speak again.

'I apologise if you think I treated you unfairly.' Leigh sounded as if the words had had to be dragged from him. 'Steve has convinced me that my suspicions were unfounded.'

'Steve has convinced me'! For a moment Jassy closed her eyes against the pain that ripped through her. If this was an apology, then she would infinitely have preferred it if Leigh had stayed angry. At least then he was being honest!

Drawing on all her strength, Jassy folded her hands on top of her typewriter. Still not looking at Leigh, knowing it would destroy her composure to do so, she stared at a patch of carpet some yards from her desk and said in a cold, proud voice that matched Leigh's own, 'If that is the best you can do in the way of an apology, Mr Benedict, then I suppose I shall have to accept it. But I have to tell you that I find it totally inadequate.'

Out of the corner of her eye she saw how Leigh's hands clenched tightly at his sides and she tensed inwardly, waiting for the inevitable explosion, but, surprisingly, it never came. Leigh remained silent, towering over her in a way that made her feel frighteningly vulnerable. Unable to see his face, she could not judge his mood, and she desperately wished that he would say something. But when he did, it was not at all what she had expected.

'You could at least look at me!' Leigh's voice was suddenly inexplicably husky. 'How can I talk to you when I can't even see your face?'

Jassy's control almost deserted her. She was too aware of the new discoveries she had made about herself to be able to see him looking as she knew he must look now, with the black anger darkening his face, cold contempt in his eyes.

'Jassy?' There was a new, questioning note in Leigh's voice, one she had never heard before. 'Jassy, look at me, for heaven's sake!'

Mutely Jassy shook her head, but even as she did so strong fingers caught hold of her chin, stilling the movement and lifting her face to meet his searching gaze.

'What's this? Tears?'

Leigh's finger brushed her cheek where, unknown to her, a single tear had escaped and trailed a glistening path down her cheek. In spite of the gentleness of his touch, Jassy jumped as if she had been burned, and pulled away.

'Yes, tears!' she flung at him. 'Don't tell me you've never made a woman cry before!'

'No more than any other man,' Leigh responded with a flash of his old sardonic humour. 'Even Steve's caused a few tears in his time.' Abruptly his expression sobered again. 'I never meant to hurt you,' he said and his eyes had a strange, stunned expression as if he had just been hit very hard.

'Didn't you? You had me tried and condemned before I could even say a word in my own defence. You thought——'

'Well, what the hell was I supposed to think?' Leigh exploded fiercely, gripping the edge of the desk with such force that Jassy fully expected to see the wood splinter beneath the pressure of his fingers. Suddenly he swung away from her, pushing his hands violently through his hair, ruffling its bright sleekness. 'Dear lord!' he said flatly. 'What are you doing to me?'

Without warning he slumped down in a chair, his head in his hands, looking thoroughly defeated, and at the sight of him suddenly so still, so unlike the Leigh she knew, Jassy's heart twisted inside her, her anger fading swiftly.

'What am *I* doing?' she managed shakily. 'I think it's the other way round. What are *you* doing to me? Why do you always want to believe the worst of me? Why won't you believe me when I tell you that I don't give a damn who you are, that . . .' Her voice faded as she realised just what she was saying.

Leigh's head came up at her words, and as he tossed a lock of hair out of his eyes Jassy thought she saw a flash of his old fire burning deep in them, but mixed with something else, an intensity of raw emotion that she could not understand at all.

'I want to believe you,' he said huskily. 'I want you so much that I reckon I'll go completely insane if I don't get you. I'm half demented as it is, just being with you——'

At Jassy's sharply indrawn breath he stopped abruptly, his head inclined slightly to one side as if he was listening to his own words over again inside his head.

'Oh, hell,' he groaned, the wry smile tinged with self-derision that accompanied his words dangerously appealing, and Jassy could not help responding to it.

'That wasn't quite what you meant to say?' she teased softly.

'No,' Leigh admitted ruefully. 'I meant to leave that side of things out of this.'

He regarded Jassy with dark, serious eyes, then suddenly the corners of his mouth quirked up and the familiar wicked glint lit his eyes.

'But now that I have said it, I'm damn glad! I couldn't have gone on much longer without saying it. Jassy——' his voice was soft and enticing as he held out his hand to her '—come here.'

Jassy knew it was foolish to give in so quickly, it was possibly even downright dangerous, but she might as well have asked a needle not to be drawn to a magnet. As if in a dream she crossed the room, the narrow stretch of carpet between them suddenly seeming very, very wide. As soon as she was within reach Leigh caught her hands and pulled her down beside him. He took her face between his hands and rested his forehead against hers.

'I'm *sorry*,' he said softly. 'Please forgive me.'

A tiny flame of anger still burned in Jassy's mind as she struggled against the hypnotic spell he was weaving.

'A little better than your last attempt,' she said sharply. 'I suppose you think this makes it all right, wipes out all those accusations!'

'No!' The word was almost a groan, stilling the flow of angry words. 'Jassy, I'm sorry,' Leigh whispered huskily. 'Sorry—sorry—sorry.'

He punctuated the words with gentle kisses and Jassy knew she was lost, all the fight seeping out of her as he pulled her up against him.

'I know my temper's foul, but I wasn't thinking straight—I find it very hard to be rational where you're concerned. I wanted to believe you were different, that you weren't like all the others—I didn't know how much I wanted that until I realised how it felt to think that perhaps, after all, you had been using me. Then I just went completely crazy.'

Leigh stirred slightly, looking down into Jassy's face, and, seeing how his eyes were once more darkly serious, Jassy was reminded of how, earlier, she had wondered if there was more than just his experiences with Gemma Morgan and her type behind his feelings.

'Am I forgiven?'

There was no way Jassy could have said no if she'd wanted to, for, as she lifted her head, his mouth came down on hers in a long, lingering, and yet strangely tentative kiss. As he drew her even closer, his strength lifting her off the floor, Jassy put her arms around him, holding him very tightly, a faint sigh of contentment escaping her. She knew there was no future in it—she would be deluding herself if she asked for any such thing—but she also knew that she no longer cared. She wanted Leigh so much that if he would only hold her like this, kiss her until all rational thought was driven from her mind, then she could be content.

At last, reluctantly, Leigh released her, one hand still lingering in the tumble of pale hair at the back of her neck.

'You, young lady, are a very bad influence,' he said in husky mock reproof. 'I am supposed to be working.'

'So am I,' Jassy reminded him mischievously, relaxing in the warmth of the laughter in his eyes. 'You're paying me overtime, remember?'

'Am I indeed? In that case, you'd better start earning it. Come on——' Leigh got to his feet, pulling Jassy up beside him '—let's have that efficient secretary back again—and I suppose we'd better tell Steve it's safe to come in. I suspect he's staying tactfully out of the way.'

His attention was already drifting away towards his desk, but just as Jassy struggled with the pang of disappointment she felt at his swift change of mood he shot her a dark-eyed sidelong glance.

'But don't bury the lover too deep,' he said in a voice that was a promise and a husky enticement rolled into one. 'I shall want her again later.'

A short time later, it was as Jassy had known it would be. Concentrating on what he was doing, Leigh hardly spared her a second glance, the moments she had spent in his arms apparently wiped from his mind—but this time it was different from the way things had been the day before.

Without being quite sure how it had happened, she realised that the three of them, Leigh, Steve and herself, had become a team, each with their own particular contribution to make to the project that absorbed them all. There was a unique satisfaction in being able to put her hands on any document Leigh wanted, sometimes even before he had asked for it because, in spite of the fact that she was busy typing up the script, she was constantly alert to the discussion between the two men on the other side of the room, and she found she was able to sense the way Leigh's mind was working, knowing instinctively just what he would need. Even the mundane process of typing page after page took on a new dimension because it was an essential part of the process to which she was now as whole-heartedly committed as Leigh himself.

And if occasionally, as she worked, she felt a pang of regret at the thought that the part of Clara could never be hers, she pushed it away ruthlessly. Clara was a wonderful role, but there would be other parts, other plays, perhaps even other films. There was only one Leigh Benedict and, right now, he was all she cared about.

CHAPTER SIX

'LEIGH! I didn't expect to see you tonight.'

'I didn't think I'd be free, either.' Framed in the doorway of Jassy's flat, Leigh looked tired, his tawny eyes shadowed. 'But I got the interview over sooner than I expected, and—can I come in?'

'Of course.'

Released from the surprise of his unexpected late arrival, Jassy held the door open. Moving into the room, Leigh flung himself on to the settee, stretching his legs out in front of him with a sigh.

'Lord, but I'm tired!' he exclaimed. 'And, as you know, interviews are not my favourite occupation.'

Jassy barely heard him, she was still trying to adjust to the fact that he was here, in her flat, for only the second time, something that brought home to her just how short a time she had known him.

It had been a strange week. After the intensity of the previous Sunday there seemed to have been a sort of hiatus, a pause in the development of their relationship. It was as if, having admitted to the desire he felt for her, Leigh had needed time to adjust to what had happened, almost as if he was as stunned by his outburst of three days ago as Jassy herself had been. At work things were very much the same. Leigh was no easier to work for—in fact, it seemed as if the idea of *Valley of Destiny* absorbed him more than ever, and he drove Jassy and Steve—and himself— harder than ever, so that at times it seemed that that passionate declaration had never been made.

But Jassy knew it had, and as a result everything Leigh did, every word he spoke to her was imbued with a new significance. At times she would look up to find his eyes on her, or he would flash his wide, devastating smile and a glowing heat would suffuse her body so that she felt she were in the grip of a raging fever, but he had made no move to take matters any further.

He had simply declared that he wanted her, that he could wait for her, and left it at that. But how long could this waiting time go on? How long would it be before Leigh would press her for a response—a response that she wasn't entirely sure she could give him? Physically, she wanted him as much as he wanted her, but emotionally she still wasn't sure, and that waiting time had given her too many chances to think, to consider the possible repercussions for herself if she embarked on a relationship that she wasn't at all certain she knew how to handle.

'Are you going to stay there all night?' Leigh enquired curiously. 'And why do you look as if you've never seen me before in your life?'

'I'm sorry.' Jassy jerked into life, closing the door hastily.

This was crazy! Ever since Leigh had left the office, heading for yet another interview with a journalist from a women's magazine, she had found herself missing him intolerably, but now that he was here with her she felt restless and unsettled, like a cat on hot bricks. She was also painfully conscious of the fact that the blue cotton robe she had put on after a bath was well past its best. Worn for comfort rather than glamour, the robe was thin from repeated washing, so that in certain lights it was practically transparent—a fact that had clearly not escaped Leigh's notice as his eyes lingered on the soft curves of her body beneath the flimsy covering.

'I thought you were busy tonight,' Jassy said awkwardly, cursing the warm colour that flared in her cheeks.

'I am,' Leigh told her bluntly. 'I really shouldn't be here, but I had to unwind——'

'Then perhaps you'd like a drink.' Nervousness made Jassy break in on him clumsily. Then, remembering the pitiful state of their laughingly labelled 'drinks cabinet', she added ruefully, 'I'm afraid cider's all we've got.'

'Cider will be fine,' Leigh assured her. 'Anything—if you'll just sit down.'

'Did the interview not go very well?' Jassy asked in an attempt to make conversation when, with the drinks poured, she curled up in one of the shabby armchairs, trying to force her racing pulse to slow, her breathing to become more natural.

'We talked about the film, which I suppose has to be an improvement on the usual questions——' Leigh's mouth quirked up suddenly at the corner into an engagingly boyish lop-sided grin '—which is a pity because I was prepared for the old routine—I had my answers all ready.'

'All the important subjects?' Jassy found herself relaxing in the warmth of his smile.

'All of them,' Leigh confirmed with mock gravity. 'And she didn't even want to know.' The grin reappeared, wider this time. 'For your information, I never eat breakfast, I'm hopelessly addicted to old Beatles' records, and you've seen my car—so what else do you want to know?'

His humorous tone dispelled the last of Jassy's tension, washing it away on a rush of delight at the fact that he had remembered their conversation of the previous Friday night, happiness and relief combining in a heady mixture. Leigh was openly flirting with her, and flirting was something she knew how to handle; it was a bit like acting in a way. She heard her voice pitched at just the right level of airy insouciance as she answered him.

'I think that tells me everything about you,' she said, and was rewarded by the warm sound of his laughter.

'And what about you?'

'Oh, I was brought up never to leave the house without a good breakfast inside me, I love folk music, and I don't have a car—I can't even drive.'

'So now we know all about each other and not a point of contact in sight. It makes me wonder what I'm doing here.'

'Drinking rather flat cider,' Jassy said flippantly, and knew from the way his mouth twisted that it was the wrong answer. Her light-hearted mood slipped away from her as she blundered on thoughtlessly. 'I know it's not your usual scene—an exclusive restaurant and vintage champagne must be more your sort of thing.'

As soon as she'd spoken she wished she could cut out her foolish tongue as she remembered Anna Golden's 'very special reunion...a quiet meal, and some excellent champagne.' She saw the flash of anger deep in Leigh's eyes, the way his jaw tightened, and her grip on her glass was unsteady as she waited for the volcano to erupt.

'You've been reading too many magazines,' Leigh said tautly. 'Try again.'

Try again? She didn't know how to! He had snatched the script away from her and she didn't even know the plot of the play!

'You like rather flat cider?' she asked slightly breathlessly, and felt the frantic racing of her heart ease as Leigh answered evenly.

'Steve and I drank nothing else for years.'

'While listening to old Beatles' records?'

'Of course. Only they weren't that old then; it's quite a time since I was eighteen.' For a moment Leigh stared down into his glass, then, when he spoke again, he had unexpectedly changed the subject. 'You said you have brothers and sisters?'

'Two brothers and a sister.'

Jassy's tone was uneasy. Leigh's question had made her think of the conversation she had had with Steve when he have given her a lift home earlier that evening.

'I'm glad you and Leigh have sorted things out,' Steve had said. 'I'd hate to see two people I like—and who obviously like each other——'

His tone had made it evident that 'like' was an understatement, causing Jassy to stiffen in sudden tension. Were her feelings—and Leigh's—so very obvious?

'—torn apart over nothing. I know Leigh was out of order, but I did warn you about his temper—and, let's face it, experience has taught him that it's not wise to trust too easily.'

Gemma Morgan and her type again, Jassy had thought to herself, coming up hard against how little she actually knew about Leigh.

'He's not an easy man to get to know,' she'd said cautiously.

'He's very much the cat who walks by himself,' Steve had agreed. 'But then he's had plenty of practice. He's been on his own all the years I've know him. We met at school—Leigh was at Pinehurst then.'

A memory had floated to the surface of Jassy's mind and she had felt suddenly as if she were on a roundabout spinning out of control.

'There were some letters from there—from a children's home,' she'd said, her voice sliding up and down in the most peculiar way. Steve had nodded slowly.

'Leigh lived there for eight years, and he still keeps in touch. The staff like him to visit—he's living proof that it's possible to make a success of life in spite of a messed-up childhood. His mother——' Steve had caught himself up hastily. 'No, that's Leigh's story—if he wants to tell it.'

Jassy had shifted uncomfortably in her seat, painfully aware of the way she had dismissed Leigh as a man who had never known a moment's insecurity in his life. She couldn't imagine how she would cope without her own close-knit family. She and her parents might disagree over her choice of career, but she knew that if ever she really needed them they would be there. It seemed that Leigh had never known such love and support, but his arrogant self-confidence hid every sign of the boy Steve had been talking about—except once, she had realised, in the car when he had given her a lift home on Saturday night. Then, just the once, the public mask he wore had slipped briefly at the mention of his parents, revealing the more vulnerable inner man.

'He never talks about his past,' she'd said slowly, recalling how swiftly Leigh had clammed up again after that one brief comment about his parents.

'No, that's not his way. The past's irrelevant as far as he's concerned. He's got to the top through a combination of talent and damned hard work, and he's going to make sure he stays there. Leigh's not one to rest on his laurels; there's always one more mountain to climb, each one higher than the last.'

And *Valley of Destiny* was the latest challenge, Jassy had thought, Steve's comments reinforcing a conviction that had already been growing in her mind. The almost obsessive concentration and untiring energy that Leigh put into his work on the new film, together with all she knew about his meteoric career, marked him out as a man to whom success was everything. Perhaps that past wasn't as irrelevant as he claimed, because in his determination to put it behind him he was, as Steve had said, still looking for other mountains to climb.

Leigh's jaded comments, dismissing the awards he had already won as unimportant, showed that nothing satisfied him for very long before he moved on to something new. There was a bitter taste in Jassy's mouth as she was forced to wonder how long the attraction he felt for her would last. How long would it be before he tired of her too, and moved on to fresh conquests?

So now, with the memory of Steve's talk of Leigh's lonely childhood in her mind, Jassy's voice was slow and hesitant as she spoke about her own family.

'There's Philip, Linda, Tony and me. Phil's an architect, and Linda and Tony are both following in Dad's footsteps as doctors—he's as pleased as Punch about that.'

It was impossible to erase the faint thread of wistfulness from her voice. Perhaps one day her father would be as proud of her as he was of the rest of his children.

'And your family wanted you to do something similar.' Leigh's comment, his tone, showed that he had caught the slight unevenness in her voice. 'I can see why you had problems convincing them that acting was worthwhile. I was an only child myself, so there were no comparisons—no favourites.'

Leigh's voice had changed perceptibly on the last comment, a harsh note creeping into it, and Jassy held her breath, waiting to see if he would go on. But he volunteered no further information and, wanting to fill the uneasy silence that had descended, Jassy rushed on, 'The trouble with being the youngest of a big family is that everyone still thinks of you as the baby. I think that's why my parents were so horrified at the thought of their little girl venturing into such a precarious way of life. I'm not sure they've really quite accepted that I've grown up.'

Leigh turned to look at her once more, a smile tugging at the corners of his mouth.

'You *look* like a little girl, curled up like that.'

Jassy was lifting her drink to her lips as he spoke, and at his words she hesitated, eyeing him across the top of her glass in mock indignation.

'Is that how *you* think of me?'

'You know damn well it isn't,' Leigh responded softly, his tone bringing a warm glow to her cheeks. Leaning back in his seat, he frowned briefly and shifted slightly on the battered settee.

'Uncomfortable?' Jassy enquired archly, all her restraint and unease vanishing in the warmth of his tone.

'You bet I am!' Leigh replied feelingly. 'I'd swear this is the most uncomfortable piece of furniture I've ever encountered.'

He moved again and an ancient spring twanged loudly, sending Jassy into a fit of giggles.

'Not quite what you're used to, is it?'

Leigh's eyes were once more disturbingly direct. 'I'm not complaining—or rather——' his voice changed subtly, deepening sensually '—I won't if you come and share this archaic instrument of torture with me. It will take the weight of two people, won't it?'

Jassy nodded, stifling the giggles that were partly due to relief at the way the awkward moment had passed so easily.

'I think so,' she said slightly breathlessly. She had forgotten the effect cider had on her. After only a few mouthfuls she felt light-headed, giddy, and very, very happy—or perhaps it was not just the cider that was going to her head.

She sobered slightly when she saw the look in Leigh's eyes as he held out his hand to her, one finger beckoning her towards him, and suddenly to be with him, to feel his arms around her, was all she wanted in the world, driving all her earlier doubts and uncertainties from her head. Without hesitation she got up and moved to the settee, sitting beside Leigh and pulling her legs up on to the faded cushions. As she leaned her head against Leigh's chest she heard his deep sigh.

'That's much better,' he said contentedly, burying his face in her hair and inhaling deeply. 'You smell delicious. There's something very

erotic about freshly washed hair, not to mention
that particular glow about a woman who's just
got out of a warm, relaxing bath.'

His arms came round Jassy, his hand cap-
turing hers, playing idly with her fingers, his
touch setting her skin tingling. His mouth was
against her hair, his warm breath stirring it softly
as he slid down against the cushions so that Jassy
was half lying across him with the powerful
muscles of his thighs against her back.

'Tell me,' Leigh said after a moment, 'what
happened to that incredible pink garment you
were wearing on Sunday?'

'Oh, that.' Jassy leaned her head back so that
she could meet his eyes, seeing them glow like
polished bronze as she smiled up into them
happily. 'Do you like it? If I'd known you were
coming I'd have worn it specially.'

She heard Leigh's deep, rich laughter and her
heart soared as his arms tightened round her.

'You'll make me spill my drink!' she protested,
only half seriously.

'To hell with your drink!' Leigh growled,
taking it from her and putting it firmly down on
the floor beside his own. Then he lay back against
the soft cushions, pulling Jassy down with him.
'I didn't come here to drink cider, and you damn
well know it!'

Every trace of laughter fled from Jassy's mind
as he pulled her close, curving her body against
the hard length of his, one long-fingered hand
brushing the hair back from her face. She lay
submissive in his arms, knowing that this was

what she wanted, that she had only to wait, happy to enjoy the anticipation of his kiss.

She did not have to wait very long. A second later, Leigh's mouth was on hers, moving sensually against her lips, sweeping her away to that dreamlike world where nothing existed but herself and this one man. As his hands slid down her back she could feel their warmth through the thin cotton of her robe, and her flesh seemed to burn as if his gentle touch had scorched a path down her body. With a small, wordless sound she nestled closer, shuddering with pleasure as Leigh's mouth moved down the side of her neck to the opening of her robe, her hands tangling in the golden crispness of his hair as she sighed his name aloud.

'You're beautiful,' Leigh whispered huskily against her throat, and hot tears of happiness pricked at Jassy's eyes so that her lashes were wet when his lips brushed them a moment later.

'Jassy?'

Leigh's voice was softly questioning, his hands still for a moment, but Jassy made a soft murmur of protest, pulling his head down to hers so that their lips met once more.

His hands were more urgent now, pulling impatiently at her robe, but when his fingers closed over her breasts they were suddenly gentle again, caressing the soft flesh with a slow sureness that had Jassy arching against him, murmuring her pleasure incoherently. Seconds later, his lips were where his hands had been and Jassy's voice was silenced, her heart seeming to stand still in delight. She was scarcely breathing, conscious only of the aching need deep inside her that only Leigh could assuage. She wanted him to love her, needed him so desperately that she cried out in pain and disappointment when he moved away from her abruptly, lifting his head, his body suddenly very still.

'Leigh——' she began, but Leigh laid a finger over her lips to silence her.

And then she heard what had alerted him—the faint sound of footsteps in the hall.

'Sarah?' Leigh questioned softly, and Jassy nodded silently, almost weeping with disappointment as Leigh stood up, straightening his shirt and smoothing his ruffled hair.

His actions made Jassy aware of her own dishevelled appearance and she scrambled hastily to her feet, pulling the crumpled, unfastened robe into some semblance of order. Silently Leigh reached for her hairbrush which lay on the coffee-table, and handed it to her.

They were only just in time. While Jassy was still tugging the brush through the worst of the knots in her tangled mane of hair she heard Sarah's key in the door.

'Good evening, Cinderella.' Sarah was alone, evidently Jamie had decided to go back to his own flat that night. 'You should have come with us, we—oh!'

She stopped, startled as she noticed Leigh, who had retrieved his glass from the floor, moved to an armchair, and was calmly drinking cider, looking for all the world as if he had been sitting quietly in the same position all evening.

'Not so much of the Cinderella, I see!' Sarah declared with a knowing glance at Jassy's pink cheeks. 'Hello, Leigh. I didn't expect to see you here tonight. Don't tell me you two have been working this late.'

'Not working, no,' Leigh answered with an easy smile. 'And I was just going.'

How could he look so calm and collected? Jassy wondered. She still felt distinctly shaky after the abrupt change of mood, and the ache of longing that Leigh's interrupted lovemaking had caused would not go away. But, of course, she was forgetting what a consummate actor he was, able to turn on any mood at will. Underneath that controlled exterior he was probably as shaken as she was.

Or was he? Glancing at Leigh's smiling face, Jassy was forced to wonder just which was the role and which was the real Leigh. Had the passionate lover, a part he had played to perfection so many times before, been the truth, or was it just another carefully assumed mask? Or had Leigh simply not felt the intensity of desire that she had experienced herself? Inwardly Jassy sighed. Was she always going to be plagued with these doubts where Leigh was concerned?

'Oh, don't let me drive you away.' Sarah's Cheshire Cat smile jarred painfully on Jassy's hypersensitive nerves. 'I was going to make some supper if you'd like some—I'm starving.'

'Not for me, thanks.' Leigh stood up, setting his glass down on the coffee-table. 'I have a long day ahead of me tomorrow, and I could do with an early night for once. Well, earlyish,' he added with a rueful glance at the clock.

He was turning towards the door as he spoke, and Jassy took a step to follow him, then hesitated, conscious of Sarah's eyes on her.

'Don't bother to see me out,' Leigh told her. 'About tomorrow—I don't expect to be in before five, but if anything urgent crops up Steve will know where to find me.'

He touched Jassy's cheek, very lightly, very briefly.

'See you,' he said softly, then he was gone, and as Jassy heard his swift footsteps descending the stairs she felt that the flat suddenly seemed very cold and empty without him. The light-hearted, giddy mood had gone completely, leaving her with a sense of dissatisfaction and discontent. She felt as flat as her half-finished glass of cider, still standing on the floor where Leigh had placed it, and her body still ached in bitter frustration at the abrupt end to Leigh's lovemaking.

'Well I'm glad to see that you two have buried the hatchet,' Sarah said, dropping her handbag on the settee and shrugging herself out of her jacket. 'You were like a bad-tempered terrier on Sunday, snapping and snarling at Leigh all the time—but you didn't fool me with all that "I don't like him" business. I thought you were only playing hard to get. Have you slept with him?'

Jassy shook her head, reflecting wryly that her friend had never been one for beating about the bush.

'Has he asked you to? Of course he has,' Sarah answered her own question. 'Well, he'll not *ask* again. He's not the asking kind—he's a taking sort of man. I doubt if he'll take no for an answer a second time.'

'I won't be saying no,' Jassy said quietly, bringing Sarah's head round sharply. Her own mind reeled as she heard what she had said, the certainty in her tone. She was stunned to find herself suddenly totally emotionally convinced of something that she couldn't remember ever having made a rational decision about.

'I *see*. He really has bowled you over, hasn't he? And what about your precious hobbyhorse— success by merit and all that? How does that affect your relationship with Leigh?'

'Nothing's changed.' Jassy's tone was a little sharp, because if the truth were told she hadn't stopped to consider that particular aspect of things. 'That won't alter anything,' she went on more quietly. 'My relationship with Leigh is quite separate from my work, and I intend to keep it that way.'

And that was the way Leigh would want it too, she added in the privacy of her own thoughts. He was never likely to offer her *anything* in the way of work—other than as his secretary, of course— because he'd shown himself to be even more op- posed to the casting-couch syndrome than she was

herself—and with good reason, she acknowledged, thinking of Gemma Morgan.

Even as she accepted that that was the way
things would be, for one split second Jassy's am-
bitions as an actress warred with her belief in personal integrity, but in the end it was no real
contest. From the moment she had realised that
Leigh felt as strongly as she did about such things,
her own convictions had been strongly reinforced,
and even if he were to offer the part of a
lifetime—and the role of Clara was just that—
she knew she would have to refuse it. And deep
down inside she also knew that she wouldn't have
it any other way. Right now, what she had with
Leigh was more important than any career
success.

But what about Leigh? What exactly did he feel
for her? He had made his desire for her only too
plain, but was there anything more than that? He
had offered no word of commitment, but then
she had never expected that. Leigh's commitment, his dedication, was given to his work—
even Anna Golden seemed to have drifted in and
out of his life, with Leigh sparing her what little
time and energy were left after the demands of
his career. The older woman seemed to be able
to accept that, or at least had learned to tolerate
it, but could Jassy?

And what did Leigh plan to do about Anna?
During the past week, the older woman's name
had never been mentioned, nor, to Jassy's
knowledge, had Leigh contacted her in any way,
but, equally, he had never actually said that his

affair with the actress was over, and Jassy knew that she would be deceiving herself if she tried to pretend that that didn't matter. She had to face facts, and the fact was that any involvement with Leigh Benedict was probably very unlikely to last, that in the end it would bring as much pain as pleasure.

But another fact was that Jassy was already involved. Leigh was what she needed *now*. Even if it would be safer, less painful in the long run, to stop now, with her heart and her body still intact, she knew she couldn't do it. The one thing she could not deny was the physical passion that flared between herself and Leigh, and if that passion was all that he had to give, then at least she would have had that, and the prospect of even a brief idyll of such delight seemed infinitely preferable to the certainty of emptiness and despair without Leigh in her life at all.

CHAPTER SEVEN

LEIGH'S house seemed strangely deserted when Jassy let herself in the next morning. Even though Steve, already busy at his desk, called out a cheery welcome as Jassy passed his door, his friendly presence did nothing to dispel the sense of emptiness that oppressed her simply because Leigh wasn't there. Throughout the day she was always conscious of the empty desk on the other side of the room, and had to force herself to concentrate on her work. Her abstracted mood was so obvious that Steve commented on it when they shared a snack lunch together.

'Are you sure we haven't been working you too hard? You had no free time at all at the weekend, remember? We must owe you a couple of days off. Why don't you stay at home tomorrow? I'll square it with Leigh. We're going to be tied up all day with these wretched auditions, so there won't be anything going on here. You could go and blow some of the overtime money we're paying you—you've earned it.'

A day off seemed like an excellent idea, Jassy reflected. Perhaps some time on her own, away from Leigh's forceful presence, would give her a chance to think things through, work out just how she really felt about this situation that had blown up like a tropical storm, sweeping her off what she had formerly believed was her steady, well-thought-out path through life. And she would have found it very difficult to cope, being here on her own, knowing that somewhere, at the auditions that Steve and Leigh had organised, other actresses would be testing for the part she so longed to play.

The crawling hands of the clock had finally made their way round to half-past four when the office door opened, making Jassy's heart leap in a way that made a mockery of her earlier belief that she had anything to think through where Leigh was concerned. He was only half an hour early, but her delight at even that tiny reprieve from the emptiness of the day told her how much he had come to mean to her in the short time she had known him.

Her spirits plummeted again violently as she looked up into a pair of cold green eyes, dramatically emphasised by the heavy application of darker green eyeshadow and thick black mascara. Numbly Jassy became aware of the gleaming red hair, the voluptuously curved body in a stunningly simple cream silk dress, as Anna Golden stalked into the room.

'Can I help you, Miss Golden?' Jassy's voice sounded weak and constrained, revealing the effort she was making to sound polite and uninvolved, while her stomach was twisting itself into painful knots of apprehension at the thought of what the actress was doing in Leigh's home.

'I'm afraid Mr Benedict is out at the moment, but——'

She broke off abruptly as Anna raised a heavily ringed hand to silence her in a gesture as imperious as that of some absolute ruler dealing with her lowly subjects.

'Spare me the pleasantries, please. I know exactly where Leigh is—it was you I came to see.'

'Me?'

Anna smiled nastily at Jassy's evident astonishment.

'Yes, you, Miss Richardson. I came to see what you were like.' The actress's tone made it plain that, now that she had seen Jassy, she was not at all impressed. A tiny frown crossed her forehead. 'I've seen you before, haven't I?'

'At Julio's.' Recalling that meeting, Jassy wasn't at all surprised that Anna didn't remember her clearly. She had been more concerned with herself and the message she had wanted passing on to Leigh. A feeling like a knife being twisted deep inside made Jassy wince as she remembered the content of that message.

'Now,' Anna clearly wasn't interested in where she had seen Jassy before, or when, 'perhaps you can tell me where Leigh was last night?'

'He had an interview—you must know that—and then——' Jassy broke off abruptly, disturbed by the vindictive flash in Anna's green eyes.

'It's that "and then" that concerns me. I had arranged a dinner party last night, a dinner to which some very special people had been invited, and Leigh had promised to be there, but he didn't turn up. We waited for him for hours, then just after ten he rang to say that something important had cropped up and he wouldn't be coming after all. This morning I discovered what that "something important" really was.' The cat's eyes darkened swiftly in anger. 'He was with you!'

The swift lifting of Jassy's heart at hearing that vital 'something important' restored some of the confidence that Anna's sudden appearance and unexpected attack had drained from her.

'I think you're talking to the wrong person. Naturally, I'm sorry if your dinner party was spoiled, but I had nothing to do with that. If you have any quarrel with anyone, then it must be with Leigh himself.'

Anna's vicious smile surfaced again. 'Oh, I've no quarrel with you—I just came to warn you. I know what's happening to you; I've seen it all before. You think you're in love with Leigh, but you ought to know that he'll never love you back. Leigh isn't capable of love. Don't take my word for it—ask any woman who's been fool enough to get involved with him. Not one of them has ever touched his heart. I've no doubt he makes you feel very special——' This time Anna's smile was one of pure sensual triumph. 'He's a most accomplished lover, as I'm sure you've already discovered—definitely ten out of ten. But the truth is that Leigh has never been faithful to any woman in his life. He's greedy, you see, he can't be content with one when there are so many all ready to fall into his hands like ripe little plums just because of who he is. Oh, I grant you that you might appeal to him just now—you have an uncomplicated attractiveness that would tempt his rather jaded appetite—but when the bloom's worn off he'll discard you like a broken toy and never give you another thought. If you're lucky—and clever—if you don't cling too hard, you might last a few months, but after that——'

'I think you've said quite enough,' Jassy broke in sharply. Anna's tirade had washed over her head like a tidal wave, but one thing the actress had said had struck home, like an arrow hitting a target. All she wanted was to go somewhere quiet and think, but there was no chance of that until the other woman left. 'I'd appreciate it if you left now.'

'Certainly. I've said all I wanted to say—and I think I've made my point. But I'll warn you——' suddenly Anna's voice changed and Jassy had the uneasy feeling that what was coming next was what the older woman had really come to say '—your little idyll with Leigh is going nowhere. If you're wise you'll get out now before you regret it for the rest of your life.'

As the actress stalked from the room Jassy's hands clenched into tight fists, her nails digging into her palms, one phrase Anna had said echoing over and over in her head: 'You think you're in love with Leigh', 'You're in love with Leigh'. *Was* that what had happened? *Had* she been fool enough to fall in love with Leigh? It couldn't be true—could it?

But she was given no time to consider the question for at that moment she heard footsteps in the hall and, before she had a chance to realise what that meant, Leigh was in the room.

'Was that Anna's car I saw leaving?'

Leigh came to an abrupt halt in the middle of the room as he saw Jassy's pallor, her over-bright eyes.

'Jassy?' he said sharply. 'What is it?'

But Jassy could only shake her head. Stunned and bewildered as she was, she only knew that as soon as he had come into the room she had registered once more that glorious sense of excitement that simply seeing him could bring—but was that *love*?

'Jassy, tell me what's wrong. What did Anna say to you? Jassy——' Leigh's voice was quiet, but it had the force of a command '—*tell me*!'

Jassy tried to bring her mind back into focus. It wasn't easy with Leigh's eyes fixed on her face as if he could read deep into her heart, when even she had no idea what he might find there. But she had to say *something*, give Leigh some explanation for her disturbed state.

'She—she said you were her lover,' she faltered, saying the first thing that came into her head. 'That you were—very accomplished—t-ten out of ten.'

'Thank you, Anna!' Leigh muttered sardonically with a bitterly mocking salute in the direction of the door through which the actress had left. 'Would have you preferred it if she'd said I was hopeless?' he went on very softly. 'Jassy, be reasonable. I'm thirty-four; I'm a man, not a monk. You can learn a lot about women in

sixteen years—I'd be a pretty insensitive brute if
I hadn't picked up one or two "accomplish-
ments" along the way.'

'She——'

'Look——' Leigh broke in sharply '—the world
and his wife know that Anna and I had our
moment, but let's get one thing straight—she
doesn't own me, even if she tries to give that
impression. I *was* her lover and I've no intention
of denying that, but I've lived with that episode
in my life for long enough and I've still got the
name to prove it. I've been branded the Golden
Thief by the Press and the public and I've learned
to live with it, but I will *not* take it from you.
Unless you can put Anna, that nickname and the
whole bloody image behind you we'll call a halt
right now. We're on a long road to nowhere if
you don't take me for what I am. I'm making no
promises because I don't know if I can keep
them—but it has to be just you and me, Jassy.
If you're looking for that superstar, then forget
him; he doesn't exist. There's just a man called
Leigh Benedict—and if you want that then we'll
take it from there.'

'I *was* her lover . . . it has to be just you and
me . . .' Leigh's words dispersed the last of the fog
that had been clouding Jassy's mind. She still
didn't know if what she felt for Leigh was love
or anything close to it, but that didn't matter,
just as Anna no longer mattered, or anything in
the past. What mattered was right here and now,
and Leigh had offered her a new beginning. Her
head came up and she looked deep into those

tawny eyes, meeting their gaze without fear or hesitation.

'Hello, *Leigh*,' she murmured softly, and knew from the swift darkening of his eyes that he had caught the slight emphasis on his name and knew exactly what she had meant to convey.

'Hello, Jassy,' he said huskily, and was reaching for her when the door opened behind him.

'So this is what you get up to when my back is turned!' Steve declared laughingly. 'Put her down, Benedict, it's time Jassy was on her way home.'

Leigh accepted the interruption good-humouredly, only betraying his disappointment by the faintest rueful glance in Jassy's direction.

'I suppose I'd better let you go, then,' he said lightly. 'Otherwise I'll end up paying you even more time. No——'

The change in Leigh's tone stopped her as she reached automatically for her bag.

'I've got a better idea. Why don't you stay—have dinner with me?'

'I think this is my cue to leave tactfully,' Steve put in with a smile. 'I'll see you both tomorrow.'

Leigh barely noticed his friend's departure; his eyes were on Jassy's face, the intensity of his gaze making her heart miss a beat.

'You will stay, won't you?' he asked, his voice and expression suddenly very serious.

'I'd love to,' Jassy told him, a world of sincerity in her words, and Leigh's delighted smile swept the last bitter memories of Anna's visit from her mind.

'It'll be just the two of us,' he declared. 'We'll shut the door on the whole damn film world just for tonight.'

A sudden harsh light in his eyes, a tightness round his mouth told Jassy that Leigh was not just thinking of the film world in general, but of one female member of that world in particular, and she shivered faintly at the thought of the cold anger that Anna had roused in him. But a moment later Leigh seemed to have shaken off his dark mood as he smilingly led her into the kitchen to begin preparations for the evening ahead of her.

That night Jassy discovered another Leigh, a man who was open, friendly and relaxed, totally without the dangerous, ruthless streak in him that excited and yet frightened her, a man in whose company she found herself relaxing completely and thoroughly enjoying herself. Often, as she helped him prepare their meal, she would find his arm lingering around her waist or her shoulders, his hand touching hers deliberately when he passed her things, and finally, when all was ready and she sank down on the settee with a glass of sherry in her hand, Leigh sprawled beside her with a sigh of contentment, the glow that lit his eyes sending a rush of happiness through her.

'Are you quite comfortable?' he asked softly, with a note in his voice that told her he was not just referring to the way she had kicked off her shoes and curled her legs up underneath her. His arm, lying across the back of the settee, very close to her shoulders, was an open invitation to move closer, one she was strongly tempted to accept, but mischievously she chose to take his question at face-value.

'Perfectly comfortable,' she assured him. 'This is such a contrast to that archaic instrument of torture we have at home,' she added with a flirtatious smile, and saw Leigh's mouth curl slowly, sharing the memory.

He didn't take up the invitation in her eyes, however, but moved suddenly to sit stiffly upright, his position implying a disturbing change of mood.

'I've been thinking,' he said quietly, and Jassy tensed, knowing from his tone that what he was about to say was somehow very important. 'I've been hunting everywhere for an actress to play Clara.'

At the mention of that name Jassy felt every muscle in her body tighten, stretching out her nerves to breaking-point, her stomach twisting painfully in apprehension as the easy, relaxed mood vanished and they moved into territory that was as dangerous as a minefield.

'What about you——?'

'No!'

Jassy's answer came swiftly, sharply. She couldn't begin to guess why Leigh was even suggesting such a thing, unless it was as some sort of test of her integrity; she just knew that there was only one possible answer.

'Not even an audition?'

Leigh sounded genuinely disappointed, and that made it even harder to answer a second time.

'Not even an audition.' The struggle she was having with her own disappointed ambition made it difficult to keep her tone firm and decisive. 'That's not what I want from you, Leigh. Why do you think I left you and Steve to make all the arrangements about tomorrow so that I don't even know where the auditions are going to be held? I don't want anything to do with it—it has to be kept totally separate from you and me.'

Wide and bright, her eyes pleaded with him to believe her, but all the same she didn't know if she felt relief or disappointment when Leigh finally nodded silently.

'I'm not Gemma Morgan!' she declared vehemently, and saw Leigh wince as she reminded him of his own cynical comments.

'Do you think I don't know that?' he growled roughly. 'And it wasn't just Gemma.'

'You told me about——' Jassy began, breaking off hastily when Leigh shook his head violently.

'Not the others—before that—when I was a kid.'

Jassy's heart lurched violently at the realisation that Leigh was close to telling her about that part of his life that he had always kept so very much to himself, that intensely private area into which he allowed only a very few, trusted people.

'Steve told me that you grew up in Pinehurst— the children's home,' she said carefully when he didn't go on, obviously finding the subject extremely difficult to talk about.

The swift, narrow-eyed glance Leigh slanted in her direction made her heart sink in the fear that she had trespassed too far, driving him away from her again. But then Leigh drew in a deep, uneven breath and pushed one hand roughly through the golden silk of his hair.

'I was ten when I went to live there, just after my mother died.'

Leigh's mouth twisted as he caught Jassy's choked exclamation of shock and sympathy.

'I told you that I never knew my father—the truth is that I doubt if even my mother knew who he was. All through my childhood I had a succession of "uncles", none of whom stayed around long, but they all had one thing in common—they all had influence in the film or theatre world, and my mother believed that they would help her up the ladder of success. Next to her, Gemma Morgan and the others were complete innocents. Each new man was the one who was going to make her a star—actors, producers, directors. The irony of it all was that none of it worked. She was never more than a bit-part actress, and in the end not even that. The spells out of work got longer and longer, and that was when she started to drink. When she died, her stomach was awash with booze and sleeping tablets.'

'Leigh!' Jassy couldn't hold back her distress and horror. 'Did she——?'

'I doubt if she meant to kill herself. It was either a complete accident or one last attempt at the big dramatic gesture that would bring the man of the moment to heel. I'm damn sure she thought she'd be found in time, and that when she was he would realise what she meant to him and offer her the part of a lifetime.'

Again came that cynical twist to Leigh's mouth that stabbed straight to Jassy's heart.

'The current "uncle" was a director. But in the end, as usual, that was one more starring role that escaped her.'

The black, sardonic tone was pure adult Leigh, but behind it Jassy could hear the child he had been then.

'And that was how I ended up at Pinehurst.'

Leigh stopped speaking abruptly, and in the silence that followed Jassy felt as if someone had shone a light into a darkened room so that she could see clearly for the first time, Leigh's distrust of actresses was not just the result of the behaviour of people like Gemma Morgan; the seeds of it had been sown long ago, when he was a child, and had been fed by his mother's behaviour, her ultimate despair, and that fact had far-reaching consequences for Jassy herself. Now she felt she was beginning to understand why he concentrated so much of his energies on his work, leaving no time for the personal relationships that seemed to lead only to disillusionment.

'Oh, Leigh, I'm so sorry. I didn't——'

Leigh held up a hand to silence her. 'No apologies, Jassy, and for heaven's sake no sympathy—I don't need either of them.' If he saw the way Jassy winced at his tone, Leigh showed no sign of it. 'I've come a long way since Pinehurst, but the time I spent there taught me one thing—

in the end there's just you, no one else. Life's what *you* make of it.'

With an abrupt movement he got to his feet.

'I think it's time we ate.' He was turning towards the door as he spoke, then suddenly swung back to face Jassy. 'What I've told you is all in the past; what matters is now. I meant what I said earlier, Jassy, it's just you and me—I won't have it any other way.'

Jassy could only nod because that was how she wanted it too, but as she watched him walk out of the room she reflected that, even though Leigh had rejected any need of sympathy, the gap between the lonely, ambitious child in the orphanage and the complex, disturbing man who was now the idol of millions was not as great as he made it out to be.

And that made her wonder once again whether the offer of an audition for the part of Clara had been the test she had suspected. Did Leigh still not trust her even now?

A sensation like the touch of tiny, ice-cold footprints trailing over her skin slid down Jassy's back at the thought of how different things could have been if she had answered Leigh's question about the audition any other way, how only a few seconds could have changed everything completely. Even though a tiny part of her still cried out at the loss of such a wonderful opportunity, she was now totally convinced that she had done the right thing. There had been no other possible answer—but now her reasons for that decision were much more complicated. Her pride, her self-respect still mattered intensely, but what was perhaps even more important was that she had to prove to Leigh that not all actresses were like those others, like his mother, Gemma, and even Anna, who Leigh had said thought she owned him.

It was vital that she did convince him because somehow, without being quite sure how it had happened, her doubts and fears had melted away. She didn't know at what point in the evening she had become certain, but when or how didn't matter. The Golden Thief, the newspapers called Leigh, and now, for Jassy, the nickname had a new significance. He was a thief indeed; he had stolen her heart, and no matter what happened it would always belong to him, and to him alone. But she was going to have to tread very carefully until she had finally won his trust. If she made one false move Leigh would walk away from her without a backward glance, rejecting the actress without a thought for the woman.

CHAPTER EIGHT

THE sound of footsteps hurrying down the stairs, the slam of the door, announced Sarah's departure for work, and Jassy, who in spite of the fact that it had been nearly two before her head had touched the pillow had been lying awake for an hour or so, waiting for her friend to leave, flung back the bedclothes, too restless to stay still any longer.

She had not felt able to face Sarah over breakfast; her thoughts were too personal and private for that. Jassy couldn't help wondering if the way she felt right now was the way some girls would feel on the morning of their wedding day—a mixture of happiness, impatient anticipation and sheer blind panic all rolled into one...

She had passed through the rest of the evening at Leigh's in a hazy dream, accepting the knowledge of her love without fear, knowing only a perfect calm as she understood the truth at last. By the time she had joined him in the dining-room, Leigh had thrown off his sombre mood and was soon laughing at some remark she made, pouring wine with a liberal hand as he did so. Throughout the meal, his conversation was as intoxicating as that wine, spiced with a dry wit

that was enhanced by the way he unconsciously
slipped into the role of the person he was de-
scribing and then resumed his normal voice
almost without being aware of it. Jassy secretly
treasured those moments, the actress in her
studying each tiny, vivid performance, watching
to see how he captured mannerisms, an accent,
a personality without seeming to stop and think.

Often during the meal she glanced up to find
Leigh's eyes on her, his gaze warm as a physical
caress, and she smiled back at him, their eyes
locking together in a suspended moment of
perfect unity that excluded the rest of the world.
In those moments she wondered if she had ever
been truly alive before. Leigh was as essential to
her now as the air she breathed, so that she
couldn't imagine how she had ever managed to
exist without knowing him—and loving him. He
had spoken no word of love himself, but she
wouldn't ask for that. She had enough for both
of them, and she would give him that for as long
as she could and then, if that was not enough to
hold him, she would let him go, knowing that her
love went with him when she no longer had the
man himself.

After the meal, they lingered in the living-room,
Jassy held tight in Leigh's arms, not moving,
rarely even speaking, content just to enjoy the
happiness of being together. At last, very reluctantly, Jassy suggested that it was time for her to
leave.

'Do you have to go?' Leigh murmured, his
cheek against her hair, one hand playing idly with
a long, pale strand of it. 'It's early yet.'

'Leigh!' Jassy protested laughingly. 'It's after midnight! I may not have to work in the morning, but you do!'

She saw his eyes darken, felt his hold on her tighten before the golden head bent and his lips captured hers. Drugged by the warmth of his body, the sweetness of his kiss, she almost missed the words he whispered against her mouth.

'Don't go,' he murmured huskily. 'Stay with me tonight, Jassy; let me love you.'

She longed to say yes, wanted it with all her heart, but the memory of everything he had said earlier, the testing offer of an audition, slid insidiously between them.

'It has to be just you and me,' he had said, and until it was truly so, until the issue of who would play Clara was finally decided—until it had been given to some other actress, Jassy admitted on a wrench of pain—she could not give herself to him as freely and openly as he asked. Only when he knew for certain that it was love and not ambition that drew her to him would she really be free to give him that love, knowing he would be able to accept it without any reservations.

But Leigh had sensed her hesitation and he got to his feet with a jarring abruptness, his face shuttered, his eyes hooded and unreadable as, not looking at her, he moved away as if he needed to put some physical distance between them. Feeling lost and bereft without the warm, protective strength of his body beside her, Jassy wanted to reach out, to touch him, but he suddenly seemed very far away from her.

'Leigh—don't——'

'I'm doing this for your own good,' Leigh cut in gruffly. 'If you're going home you go now—before I forget my promise.'

'Your promise?'

'Damn you, Jassy, I said I'd wait until you weren't afraid to say you wanted me!' Leigh declared harshly, shattering the peaceful mood of the evening.

Jassy bit her lip hard, knowing she had blundered very badly. Caught up in her own developing feelings, she had forgotten the promise Leigh had made to her. Slowly she stood up, moving to take his hand very gently, wanting to draw him back to her.

'I just need a little more time, Leigh. Please understand.'

Leigh turned to her, his eyes dark and intense, deep, unfathomable pools in a suddenly drawn face.

'Then when?' he asked urgently. 'Tomorrow? Come to me tomorrow!'

Tomorrow was a new day. Tomorrow the things he had told her about his mother would not be so fresh in her mind—tomorrow someone else would have been chosen to play Clara.

'Tomorrow,' she told Leigh softly, managing a tremulous smile. 'After all, it's really that now—would another few hours be so very long?'

Even as she spoke, the feeling of his hand in hers made her body throb with the need and longing she had felt the night before, and she knew that, were Leigh even to kiss her again, she would be unable to deny him, would yield her body and her heart up to him to cherish or destroy as he willed. But Leigh responded to her gentle teasing, a smile wiping the hard, shuttered expression from his face.

'Right now an hour seems like an eternity,' he said feelingly. 'But I reckon I'll have to be patient a while longer. Come on, woman, let me get you home to your chaste little bed, then maybe I'll even get some sleep myself. At least it'll while away a few hours.'

Peace had been restored, and they were both laughing as they left the house. But a short time later, in the darkness of the car outside her flat, Leigh turned to her and took her hand in his, hard fingers gripping it firmly.

'I want you, Jassy, but you're right—something like this shouldn't be rushed. I want you to know something—that image—the Golden Thief...'

'The sex symbol?' Jassy supplied gently when he seemed to be having difficulty finding the words he wanted.

Leigh nodded silent agreement. 'It isn't real. It's as much a fantasy as the characters I play— just a myth created by the Press and the inevitable publicity that comes with the job.'

'Are you trying to say——?'

'I'm not claiming I'm an innocent, Jassy. I told you, I'm thirty-four, and I have any normal man's appetites and needs—feelings—and in our job there's plenty of temptation, but very little commitment—and one thing I've learned is that the first without the second is a potentially lethal situation. I got caught up in that once, and once was quite enough for me to learn my lesson.'

It was too dark to see Leigh's face, but his voice told Jassy very clearly that the details of that 'lesson' were not something he cared to reveal at this time.

'When I realised what was happening I knew that the whole thing was too damn risky. Quite apart from the dangers to oneself, one plus one making two is fine, but when one and one makes three, then that's trouble with a capital T—and I have no intention of being that irresponsible.'

Jassy's silence was no longer simply because she was listening intently to every word Leigh spoke; now it had an extra dimension of shock in it. She should have thought of this herself, but the truth was that it hadn't even crossed her mind. She knew what Leigh was trying to say. Knowing what she did of his past, the way his mother—and Leigh—had paid the price for his father's irresponsibility, she could understand how he felt.

'I'd never want any child of mine to grow up without a father around, so I determined that there would be no child until I wanted the mother with me for the rest of my life. I know I've rushed you, but I want you to know that I would never let you end up in my mother's situation. You do understand that, don't you?'

Jassy could only nod silently, still too stunned by her own thoughtlessness to frame an answer. That 'until I wanted the mother with me for the rest of my life' reverberated inside her head. Just what had Leigh meant to imply by that? That she could never be that woman—or exactly the opposite? She couldn't tell, and it was too dark to see into his face and read any answer there.

'Now I'm going to let you go,' Leigh said quietly. 'I want you to think about what I've said, and if you decide—well, you know where you can find me. I'll be home around seven tomorrow—tonight,' he amended wryly.

'I'll see you then.' Jassy found her voice at last. It was all she could say, there were too many other thoughts in her mind to allow her to add anything further. But deep inside she knew that there was nothing for her to think about. One thing was certain—tonight she would be with Leigh.

Just as she turned to get out of the car Leigh caught hold of her and pulled her close, crushing her up against him until she felt that her bones might break under the pressure of his hands. He whispered the one word, 'Tonight,' in a low, intense tone that made nonsense of all his carefully rationalised arguments, and Jassy knew that there was no turning back. No matter what happened, she was committed.

It was early afternoon when Jassy returned to the flat, humming to herself as she dropped the small bundle of carrier bags on to the settee and kicked off her shoes, flinging herself into a chair with a sigh of relief. She had been tramping round the shops for hours, looking for a very special dress, and she had found it—a simple sleeveless design in a sensual silky material in exactly the same shade of pink as the nightshirt Leigh had said he liked. It was the dress she was going to wear tonight.

When the doorbell rang loudly and insistently Jassy was tempted to ignore it. She was tired, and she didn't feel like company. But the caller was clearly not going to give up, and with a sigh she opened the door then stared in astonishment at the dark, heavily built man who stood on the landing.

'Benjy! What are you doing here?'

Her former tutor was the last person she had expected to see. She had become very friendly with Benjy and his wife while she was at college, but just lately she had seen very little of them.

'I've been trying to reach you all day.' Clearly agitated, Benjy wasted no time on polite preliminaries. 'I've rung you every half-hour since nine o'clock.'

'I've been shopping,' Jassy said dazedly. 'I went out early, and I've only just got back.'

'Well, now you're coming with me. My car's outside—we can just make it if we hurry.' He was halfway out of the door as he spoke. Jassy caught hold of his arm before he disappeared completely.

'Hang on, Benjy! We can just make what? Where are we going?'

'To your audition.' Benjy's round face was glowing with excitement. 'The biggest chance you'll ever get, my girl, so stop messing about and let's get going. I'll explain on the way.'

'Now don't get yourself into a frazzle, honeybun,' Benjy soothed as they sped away from the flat. 'I couldn't give you any warning of this because I didn't get any myself—and I can't tell you a great deal because I'm sworn to secrecy about much of it, but all you need to know is that last night I had some friends round to dinner—theatre people—and we started discussing my ex-pupils and what they were doing and, of course, as one of my stars, your name came up. Well, to cut a long story short, one of my friends who has a great deal of influence with a certain producer—mentioning no names, of course—felt you would be perfect for a *very important part*——' Benjy emphasised the last three words dramatically.

'—and would you be interested? Of course, having your best interests at heart, I said you damn well would! A quick telephone call to the right people this morning wangled you an audition, then all I had to do was find you—you didn't exactly make that easy!'

'Benjy, you're an angel!'

Jassy's words came jerkily because of the excitement that seemed to be bubbling like red-hot lava in her veins. 'Theatre people,' Benjy had said, so there must be some new production coming up that even her agent didn't know about yet.

Working for Leigh had been a rewarding experience in more ways than one, but Jassy had missed acting so terribly, and her heart soared with excitement at the thought that she might soon be working at the job she loved—and possibly, to judge from Benjy's hints, in some major new play.

And there was another, secret hope that she hugged tightly to herself as the car sped through the streets. She would go to Leigh tonight, whatever happened. Loving him as she did, she *had* to go, but how much better it would be if she could also tell him that she had won an important role by her own efforts, without his help or even his knowledge. Surely then he would *know* that she loved him for himself and not because of what he could give her as an actress?

'Nearly there,' Benjy warned her, shooting round a corner at breakneck speed. 'I can't tell you anything about the part—I gave my word on that—but I can say one thing: if you get this, then you're *made*, honeybun. Just don't panic, and remember I have faith in you. You can do it if you don't lose your nerve—so just get in there and show 'em. We're here,' he added unnecessarily as the car screeched to a halt.

Not giving Jassy time to get her bearings, Benjy bundled her out of the car and into the theatre, hurrying her along a dimly lit corridor until at last they halted just out of earshot of the stage. The backstage area was crowded with girls of around Jassy's own age, one or two of whom she recognised from her years at college. But she had no time to look around her because someone had thrust a script into her hands and Benjy was giving her last-minute instructions in a low, urgent voice.

'Now get your breath and relax. I know you haven't had time to look at the script, so you'll have to listen very carefully when they tell you the plot and then take it from there.' Benjy's smile was positively paternal. 'I know you're panicking now, but you'll be all right as soon as you get on that stage—you always are.'

'Miss Richardson,' a voice was calling behind Jassy. 'Miss Richardson, please!'

Benjy gave her a firm push forwards and, her mind still reeling from the unexpectedness of everything, she stumbled towards the brightly lit stage where an actor who she vaguely recalled from a couple of television plays stood waiting to read the part through with her. In contrast to the brightness of the stage lights, the theatre auditorium was very dark. Jassy knew that there must be several people out there, but blinded by the glare of the spotlights, she couldn't see a thing.

There was a sudden silence as she appeared on stage; an inexplicable, paralysing silence that stretched Jassy's already taut nerves almost to breaking-point, so that she clutched the pages of her script even tighter as she waited. If only they would let her begin! She would feel so much better then. But still the silence went on until at last, after an unendurable wait, a different voice spoke directly to her from the darkness.

'OK, Miss Richardson, let me tell you something about this film . . .'

Film. The word was like a blow to her face, making her head spin sickeningly so that she scarcely heard the brief but comprehensive summary of the plot, the helpful insights into the character of the girl she was to play. She didn't need them anyway; she knew every last detail of the story as well as she knew the voice that had come so shockingly out of the darkness. The script she held in her tightly clenched hands was the script of *Valley of Destiny*, the voice in her ears was Steve Carter's—and if Steve was there then Leigh must be too!

White with panic, Jassy scanned the rows of seats in the auditorium, searching frantically through the blackness until at last she could just make out a gleaming blond head very dimly through the darkness.

Leigh was sitting frighteningly still, his face completely in the shadows, his white shirt in stark contrast to the gloom around him. Jassy could see nothing of his face, but it was his total immobility that terrified her. She had seen that stillness before, when Leigh was very, very angry. She longed to turn and run, go anywhere if she could only escape from the cold, hostile eyes she knew were fixed on her even if they were hidden from her sight, but she knew that if she started running she would never be able to stop. She had to go through with this audition now, though a savage pain seared through her as if her heart were slowly tearing in half.

'I realise that you haven't had time to prepare yourself,' Steve was saying, a strong note of sympathy in his voice. 'We only had your name put forward for the part this morning, so we have rather rushed you through. Would you like a couple of minutes to read over your lines?'

Numbly Jassy shook her head. She just wanted to get on with it, get it over, then she could go away and hide—if there was anywhere she could run to where Leigh would never find her.

'Quite sure? OK—whenever you're ready.'

At last Jassy found the strength to look at the script she held. She had thought that nothing could hurt any more than the pain she already felt, but the first lines that danced in front of her blurred eyes twisted the knife even deeper into her heart.

Of all the scenes in the film, the one chosen for the audition was the very scene Jassy had read aloud to herself on the night she had taken the script home, imagining herself playing Clara opposite Leigh. Now she was being given the chance to act the role she had so longed for, but the man playing Francis was a total stranger, and somewhere in the darkness of the auditorium Leigh's tiger's eyes were watching her.

Jassy could almost feel those golden eyes burning into her as she began to read, stumbling hopelessly over the words. She felt as if she were in the grip of some appalling nightmare from which she couldn't wake, but this was no dream, it was horrifyingly, terrifyingly real, and so there was no way she could even begin to think herself into the part of Clara.

In the privacy of her own flat she had known instinctively how every one of these words should be spoken. She had imagined gestures, movements, intonations, to bring out the character of the woman she was playing, but now all her ideas deserted her. She could remember none of those subtleties, could hardly even focus on the lines on the page before her. She knew that her performance was appalling, her actions wooden, her delivery almost incoherent, but she couldn't bring herself to care. She was ruining the biggest chance of her career, throwing away all hope of being cast in the part she had dreamed of, but the role of Clara, even her own future as an actress, were nothing to her if she lost Leigh—and, knowing how he must inevitably interpret her sudden appearance at the audition, she could have little doubt that after this she had lost him forever.

After what seemed like an eternity the ordeal was over. The last line had been spoken and Jassy stood miserably silent, every ounce of energy drained from her. Glancing at the actor who had read the part of Francis, she could see nothing but pity in his eyes, pity for a young, untalented girl who had made a complete fool of herself.

That was the last straw. Turning awkwardly, Jassy fled blindly from the stage and stumbled into the wings where Benjy was waiting for her.

'Jassy, honeybun, *what* came over you? That wasn't like you at all. You just went to pieces.'

Her tutor put his arm around her waist in a gesture of instinctive comfort, but Jassy didn't even notice. She was beyond comfort, beyond caring.

'Benjy, please,' she pleaded wearily. 'I can't explain, please don't ask me to.' All she wanted

to do was go, get away from the theatre, away
from Leigh. 'Take me home,' she whispered, her
voice dull and lifeless.

Behind her she heard the murmur of voices, a
faint commotion further down the corridor, and,
looking up, saw the painfully familiar tall, golden-
haired figure and knew it was too late. Leigh
shouldered his way through the crowded corridor
towards her, ruthlessly ignoring all attempts to
speak to him, roughly shaking off hands placed
on his arm to gain his attention, and Jassy knew
she was trapped. There was nowhere for her to
run to, and even as she shrank back against the
wall brutal fingers closed over her arm and Leigh
pulled her roughly round to face him. His face
was white with anger, the tawny eyes slitted and
pitiless, burning with an icy fury.

'My car's outside,' he said, and it was a
command, not a statement.

Without loosening his cruel grip on Jassy's
arm, he turned and made his way back down the
corridor, dragging her along with him. Jassy had
a fleeting glimpse of Benjy staring in shock and
bewilderment, she saw the envious faces of the
other girls, their envy changing rapidly to doubt
as they saw the grim set of Leigh's features, and
then they were at the stage door. Leigh paused
just long enough to toss a key to the doorman
before pushing Jassy out of the door and across
the street to where his car stood, unnoticed in the
confusion of her arrival less than an hour before.
Bundling her unceremoniously into the front

passenger seat, Leigh slammed the door shut after her.

It took only a few seconds for him to make his way round to the other side of the car and slide into the driver's seat, but Jassy took her chance and fumbled frantically with the door, trying desperately to open it—but it refused to move. Leigh watched her struggles silently for a moment.

'You're wasting your time. It locks automatically—you can only get out when I let you.'

He reached out a hand to pull her away from the door and, panicking at the thought of having him touch her in cold anger again, Jassy struck out at him blindly. Leigh saw the blow coming and flung up his arm to ward it off so that her fist landed impotently on sinewy muscle. Immediately afterwards, she was slammed back in her seat with a violence that drove all the breath from her body.

'None of that!' Leigh snarled. 'You've done enough damage that way already. Just sit quiet until I get you home, then you can try all the dirty tricks you like. But I warn you, I'll use a few of my own right back, so don't push me. Right now, I'm sorely tempted.'

His grip tightened bruisingly on her arm and Jassy winced in pain.

'You're hateful!' she spat the words into his face in fear and distress, wanting only to hurt him as she was hurting, but Leigh shrugged indifferently.

'We've been through all that before,' he said impassively. 'Personally, I don't give a damn what you think of me—my opinion of you is none too high either. So unless you want to have this out right here and now, where everyone can see us, I suggest you curb that shrewish tongue of yours, for a while at least. It won't take us long to get to my place—if you're wise you'll use the time to think up some new story to tell me this time.'

Abruptly he released her, turning away to start the car, jerking it into gear viciously and swinging away from the kerb at a speed that had the tyres squealing protestingly.

It was a nightmarish journey. Leigh drove with reckless abandon, as if totally oblivious of the early rush-hour traffic and they had several very narrow escapes which had Jassy's stomach contracting in panic before they reached the quiet square where Leigh's house stood. Once released from the car, Jassy stumbled inelegantly across the courtyard, propelled roughly towards the door by Leigh's hand at her back. After unlocking the door, Leigh stood back.

'After you,' he said with a mocking bow.

Defiantly Jassy shook her head. She was not going in there! She couldn't bear to be alone with Leigh here, in this house where such a short time before she had been so very happy.

'Very well,' Leigh declared calmly, and before Jassy quite realised what he had in mind he lifted her bodily from the ground and carried her, struggling frantically, into the house.

Kicking open the first door that led off the hall, Leigh strode into the living-room and deposited Jassy unceremoniously on the floor. Then as she sprawled awkwardly on the thick carpet he moved to the drinks cabinet, splashed a large whisky into a tumbler and gulped down half of it in one go.

Thinking that his attention was off her, Jassy scrambled to her feet and made a desperate dash for the door, but, quick as she was, Leigh's reactions were quicker. He reached the door just before she did and slammed it shut, leaning his broad shoulders against it and effectively preventing any further attempt at escape.

'Sit down!' he ordered, and Jassy knew that she had no alternative but to do as he said.

Leigh watched silently as she sank dejectedly into a chair, painfully and belatedly aware of the fact that her fear had driven her to act in a way that, in his mind, would confirm his belief that she was guilty, that she was afraid of facing him now that he had found out how she had been using him. As she cursed her thoughtless action Leigh reached for his glass, lifting it in a mockery of a toast before he swallowed the rest of his drink.

'Now we can talk,' he said coldly, replacing the glass on the dresser beside him. 'Tell me,' he went on, his tone a grim parody of polite interest, 'do you think you'll get the part?'

'The—the part?' Jassy echoed foolishly, her brain refusing to function properly.

She had expected anger, had nerved herself to face the savage lash of his tongue; instead she was confronted by a coolly civil stranger and she had no idea how to cope with the man Leigh had suddenly become.

'Yes, that very important part.' Leigh smiled cruelly. 'Do you think you'll get to play Clara? After all, you went to a great deal of trouble to make sure the role was yours—a magnificent performance,' he added caustically, and Jassy knew he was not referring to the black farce of her audition. 'So tell me, honestly, how do you rate your chances, Miss Richardson?'

Jassy could find no way to answer him. Every word Leigh spoke seemed to stab straight into her heart like the point of a red-hot knife. Despairingly she covered her face with her hands, but it was no use; she could still see Leigh's darkly taunting face in her mind.

'It was all going so well, wasn't it, my darling? Everything just fell into place for you. You got your hands on a copy of the script so that you could study it before everyone else, and then you went to work on me. You damn nearly succeeded too—you had me just where you wanted me!'

Leigh slammed his fist violently into the wall at his side and Jassy's head jerked up at the sickening thud as his hand hit the paintwork.

'I was crazy over you,' Leigh went on, apparently oblivious of his bruised and reddened knuckles. 'I would have done anything for you, but there was just one thing you wanted. You knew Gemma Morgan's tactics hadn't worked in the past, so you tried another way—so it was, No, Leigh, not tonight; I need more time.'

A small moan of pain escaped Jassy at Leigh's bitter mimicry of her own words. She knew how much he must be hurting inside, but his black cynicism revealed only too clearly how determined he was not to let that pain show. In this mood he would never listen to her, and she could only pray that if she allowed him to give his bitterness free rein he would eventually calm down enough to allow her to explain. Whether he would believe her explanation, she didn't know. She still couldn't believe what had happened herself.

'How far would you have gone, I wonder?' Leigh mused cynically, his head slightly on one side as if he was actually considering the question. 'If I'd been a little more reluctant—not quite so easily enslaved—would you have played your trump card? Would you have let me make love to you, Jassy, if that was what it took to get the part?'

'Leigh, please don't!' Jassy pleaded, her eyes wide dark pools in an ashen face. 'It was never like that! You've got it all wrong! I——'

'Hell, but you must have wanted that part!' Leigh cut in, his voice thick with disgust. 'What wouldn't you have done to get it? Tell me——' his voice altered suddenly, becoming strangely quiet, almost conversational in tone '—do you still want it?'

'What?' Jassy couldn't believe what she was hearing. 'What did you say?' she asked with difficulty, the words clumsy on her tongue.

'I asked if you still wanted the part of Clara.'
Leigh's unnerving calmness sent a shiver of fear
down Jassy's spine.

He was watching her intently, his narrowed eyes
making her think worriedly of a predator
watching its prey just before it sprang. In a panic
she got to her feet, backing nervously away from
him as he moved into the room towards her.

'What if I were to give it to you?' Leigh's
question was laced with silky menace. 'What
then? What are you offering in return?'

He took a step nearer and Jassy retreated
hastily, her mind whirling. He couldn't mean it!
He couldn't!

'Leigh . . .' she faltered, putting out a trembling
hand to ward him off. The tiny movement proved
her undoing; Leigh's hand snaked out and caught
her wrist, pulling her roughly up against him.

'Are you still offering your sexy little body in
return for a starring role?' he murmured, one
hand sliding down Jassy's back, tracing light,
erotic patterns over the thin cotton of her dress.
'Because if you are I might still be open to offers
if you're prepared to make it worth my while.'

If Jassy had been scared before, that fear was
as nothing when compared with what she felt
now. She was terrified, afraid of herself and for
herself because she could read what Leigh intended in his eyes and knew only too well what
would happen.

'No!' She moaned a protest, but even in her
own ears it lacked conviction. Already her trai-
torous body was betraying her, responding to

Leigh's caresses in spite of her frantic efforts to force down the aching sense of longing that filled her as soon as he touched her.

'No?' Leigh questioned softly, subtly increasing the pressure of his hands in a way that made Jassy's pulse race. 'And am I supposed to believe that you mean that?'

One hand moved to Jassy's face, Leigh's thumb slowly tracing the outline of her softly parted mouth. Her throat was painfully dry, but she found she couldn't swallow to relieve it. Why *should* he believe her? She didn't even believe herself, and Leigh had no cause to trust her ever again. She had wanted time, time to convince him that she was not like all the others, but events had caught up with her, her actions seeming to prove exactly the opposite, and now there was no time left.

'I could make you beg me to love you, Jassy,' Leigh whispered, his lips against her forehead as she closed her eyes in despair. 'It would be so easy—you see, I know exactly how to do it.'

Cradling her against the hard warmth of his body, he slid his hand downwards once more to cover one breast, making Jassy catch her breath in a devastating mixture of fear and delight.

'Because there was one thing you hadn't planned on, wasn't there, my sweet? When you set out to make me desire you, you hadn't reckoned on your wanting me every bit as much— and you do, I know you do.'

Jassy could not have denied the truth of Leigh's words if she had wanted to. Her body was acting independently of her mind, pressing close up against Leigh, her heart pounding erratically so that she knew he must be aware of the uneven tenor of her breathing. Her hands were clinging to his shoulders, her fingers clenching over the hard muscles, and unthinkingly she lifted her face to his, blindly offering him her lips.

Leigh swore hoarsely, then his mouth crushed Jassy's in a fierce, punishing kiss that forced her lips apart with its savage pressure. His fingers tightened on her breast, bruising the tender flesh so that she whimpered in pain. But a moment later she was oblivious to the cruel pressure, her mind reeling as if she were delirious. She felt as if she were on fire, the passion Leigh had unleashed in her burning her up, driving all fear or thought of her own safety from her head.

As Leigh sensed her surrender his whole body stiffened, suddenly rigid and unyielding against her. He wrenched his mouth from hers and flung her away from him, the force of his movement sending her halfway across the room.

'You disgust me!' Leigh spat the words into Jassy's white face. 'I could have had you then— you would have let me do anything I liked with you! Even now you have no shame! But you've wasted your time, my lovely Jassy; I wouldn't give you the part if you were the last actress living! How could I work with you when I can't even bear to look at you? I thought you were so different, but you're just like all the rest. How can you be so beautiful and yet so corrupt inside? Get out of here!' For the first time Leigh's voice rose to a shout. 'Get out of here and leave me in peace!'

He made a move as if he would physically throw her from the room, but Jassy had already gone. Tears blurring her eyes, she blundered through the door and out into the hall. For one terrifying moment she thought the front door was locked against her, but at last she managed to wrench it open. Then she was out of the house and running, running from Leigh as she had wanted to run as soon as she had realised his presence in the theatre, fleeing desperately, but with nowhere to go.

CHAPTER NINE

SUMMER turned to autumn and Jassy moved through her life like someone with a permanent dose of concussion, feeling as if the future was a great, dark tunnel stretching endlessly ahead without a hint of light at the end of it. London suddenly did not seem large enough to contain both herself and Leigh; she couldn't settle in her flat when any ring at the doorbell made her stomach cramp in fear that the caller might be him, and even worse was to sit alone in the silent flat, knowing that he would never call, never phone, that she would never see him again.

The one thing that kept her sane was the fact that she was working again. Only three days after the nightmare of that appalling Friday, her agent rang with the news of an audition, and to Jassy's amazement she actually got the part. How she had managed to be successful, she would never know. It seemed she must have been functioning on automatic pilot because at other times she simply went through the motions of living with a listless apathy, not feeling, drained of all energy.

But the new play was a life-saver. Jassy threw herself into the part with an intensity and commitment that drove her to the point of exhaustion, working every waking hour because that way she didn't have time to think. Somehow she got through the days, but at night, alone in her bed, she was no longer able to defend her mind from thoughts of Leigh.

Time after time she lay awake, her body throbbing with a primitive longing that made her moan aloud, afraid to sleep because if she closed her eyes she could see Leigh's face, hear his voice in her mind. Her numbed brain refused to remember that final, shattering time after the audition. It flinched away from recalling the savage anger in Leigh's eyes, the satanic mockery of his words, so that it was always the earlier, more gentle Leigh who haunted her dreams. Jassy could almost feel his touch on her skin, hear the husky intensity of his voice as he whispered, 'Stay with me tonight, Jassy; let me love you.'

Partly because of the demands of her work, but mainly because she had no inclination whatsoever to socialise, Jassy spent all her free time inside the flat in spite of Sarah's urgings that she should go out, pick up the pieces of her life and start again. So when, in late October, Benjy rang with an invitation to a party to celebrate his fiftieth birthday, she was strongly tempted to refuse.

But the party was on a Sunday, when the theatre was closed, and she knew that Benjy would be hurt if she didn't turn up, taking her absence as meaning that she held him personally responsible for the fiasco of an audition with Leigh, and so, reluctantly, she agreed to go.

She planned to arrive early, before the party really got under way, and to stay only a short time, but she knew that Benjy liked his guests to dress up so she chose a black velvet skirt and waistcoat suit worn with a white ruffled blouse, its sombre tones in keeping with her mood. As usual she wore very little make-up and left her hair loose so that it hung in gleaming waves around her face.

Early as she was, the room was already half-full of brightly clothed men and women, and Jassy stood hesitantly in the doorway, searching vainly for a familiar face in the crowd, until she heard someone call her name. Turning, she saw Benjy hurrying towards her.

'Jassy, honeybun, you look wonderful! I love the Puritan look—you make the rest of us look positively overdressed!'

Jassy's mood brightened slightly at Benjy's exuberant welcome.

'Happy birthday, Benjy! You don't look so bad yourself—in fact, you look like an enormous bumble bee in that outfit.'

'Do you like it?' Benjy spun round so that she could get the full effect of the yellow-and-black-striped shirt that did nothing to flatter his heavily built figure. 'Very me, don't you think?'

'Very,' Jassy agreed laughingly as Benjy steered her towards the drinks table and poured her a glass of wine.

'Don't run away tonight, will you, honeybun?' he said. 'I have someone very special I'd like you to meet, and if I know the lady she's bound to be late.'

Jassy's nerves, which had tightened instinctively at that 'someone very special', relaxed again at the realisation that Benjy's friend was a woman. She wouldn't have put it past her tutor to have invited her with the specific intention of trying to make amends for his failure the last time.

'Who's that?'

'Don't be impatient.' Benjy wagged a reproving finger. 'You just wait and see. I still have it in mind to do you a good turn, even if it didn't turn out quite the way I planned it the first time.'

The light faded from Jassy's eyes at his words. She had never explained what had happened at the audition, and Benjy had tactfully never pressed her for any details.

'I'm sorry I let you down, Benjy.'

'Forget it! These things happen—anyone can have an off day. Now come and meet a few people.'

Obediently Jassy followed Benjy into the crowd, acknowledging his introductions automatically with a word and a smile, but hardly registering names and faces. She felt vaguely uneasy, remembering how Benjy's earlier 'good turn' had devastated her life. She couldn't help wondering just what he had in store for her this time.

The room filled up as the evening wore on, and soon the place was packed. The air was almost unbearably warm and smoky, and Jassy felt the beginnings of a headache threaten. If Benjy's friend did not turn up soon she would have to leave, she thought, massaging her temples to ease the tension. She would wait another half-hour, no more.

She was in a quiet corner chatting to Helen Carstairs, Benjy's wife, when the door opened again and a slight commotion announced the arrival of yet another guest. Glancing automatically towards the source of the disturbance, Jassy stiffened, her face paling, her polite words dying on her lips. Anna Golden had paused deliberately in the open doorway, her action nicely calculated to give her entry the fullest possible impact and draw all eyes to her.

Not that she needed any such dramatic tricks, Jassy thought wryly. The white, clinging sheath of her dress with its deeply slashed neckline, the pagan brilliance of the heavy gold necklace around her slender throat, the glorious red hair, all made certain that no one could have missed her arrival.

As Benjy hurried forward to greet Anna, Jassy suddenly found that she was trembling all over. The actress's arrival had stunned her, but now her bemused brain was beginning to work again and her thoughts sent an icy shaft of panic down her spine. In anyone's mind, Anna Golden would always be linked with Leigh Benedict, and Jassy had foolishly forgotten that Leigh had been a student at the same drama school that she had attended. Benjy had been *his* tutor too, so wasn't it more than likely that he would have been invited to this party?

She couldn't stay, Jassy thought in a panic, her unseeing eyes still fixed on the scene in the doorway where Anna was indulgently handing Benjy an enormous parcel gaudily wrapped in shiny gold paper. She couldn't bear the thought that Leigh might arrive, that they might actually come face to face.

But then the crush around Anna and Benjy moved and shifted, a path opened in the crowd, and at the end of that path, just beside Anna, stood the man Jassy so longed and yet dreaded to see.

Leigh looked dreadful, Jassy realised with a shock as the grey haze before her eyes faded and she saw him clearly at last. His face was drawn and haggard, the shadows under his eyes giving them a faintly bruised look. He was superbly dressed as always, in a black silk shirt, black trousers and a grey velvet jacket, but the dark colour of his clothes emphasised the unnatural pallor of his face and the strained lines that were etched into it.

He looked the way she felt, Jassy thought on a pang of distress: like someone who had lost interest in everything that used to matter to him, making her remember the stories she had heard about the production of *Valley of Destiny*. It was well known that hundreds of girls had auditioned for the part of Clara, and that all of them had been rejected by Leigh, often on the slightest pretext. There were even rumours that the film would never be made, that Leigh was thinking of abandoning it or, at the very least, letting someone else direct it. That story had affected Jassy like a physical blow. Knowing how much that particular film meant to Leigh, she couldn't believe that he would willingly hand it over to anyone else.

'That's something of a triumph, isn't it?' a woman beside Jassy murmured to Helen Carstairs. 'I understood Benedict was definitely antisocial these days.'

'Leigh's been too busy to go anywhere.' There was a gently reproving note in Helen's voice. 'These problems with his film take up all his time. But he promised Benjy he'd come tonight, so I knew he'd be here. He's never let us down yet.'

What about the performance of *Romeo and Juliet*? Jassy thought unwillingly. Leigh hadn't kept his promise to Benjy then. To her consternation she found she had spoken her thoughts out loud.

'Well, you can hardly hold that against him! Benjy should have known better than to ask him to come that night—we all knew that was the day Leigh had arranged to take all the kids from Pinehurst to the seaside. It wasn't Leigh's fault if the coach broke down on the way back—and he did ring up and explain and then went straight to the college as soon as he'd got all the children safely home—but by then, of course, it was too late.'

Images were flashing through Jassy's mind like slides projected on to a screen: letters arriving at the office; Steve talking of the children's home where Leigh had lived, saying 'He still keeps in touch. The staff like him to visit'; but most of all, in heartbreaking clarity, Leigh himself, tanned and relaxed, arriving at the college, and the bitter anger she had felt towards him. She had been so swift to condemn him that day, piqued by his non-appearance at her first major performance, so that her hurt pride had blinded her to any possible explanation other than the purely selfish one she had attributed to him.

With a murmured excuse Jassy moved away, trying to blend anonymously with the mass of people in the centre of the room. Her only hope was to try to remain unseen until Leigh was no longer between her and the door and then make her escape. But Leigh showed no sign of moving. He was talking to Helen now, the harsh lines of his face softening as he smiled at her with evident affection.

For a few precious minutes Jassy allowed herself the bitter-sweet luxury of watching him, drinking in the sight of him for what she knew must be the very last time. She knew that she was only torturing herself, that the pain of loving Leigh and knowing he felt only hatred and contempt for her must inevitably be far worse after this masochistic self-indulgence, but she couldn't help herself. Seeing him there, only feet from her and yet emotionally a million miles away, it was impossible not to recall how it had felt to be so very close to him that their bodies seemed to have blended together, becoming like one person instead of two separate beings, and the memory made her blood burn with a heat that had nothing to do with the crowded warmth of the room.

Now, when she was least able to bear it, it
seemed that that heat had melted the ice that had
held her memories frozen in her mind, and images
of that last afternoon with Leigh poured into her
thoughts. She remembered his coldly calculated
caresses and her own unthinking response. She
had yielded to Leigh as she knew she would
always yield, a victim of her love for him. The
savage intensity of his disgust at her reaction was
no less painful because of the passage of time; if
anything the pain was far worse because then she
had been partially numbed by sheer shock. Now,
seeing Leigh talking to Helen with an easy
courtesy that hid the streak of explosive violence
in his character, anguish seemed to claw at Jassy's
heart, tearing it to shreds inside her.

Anna had moved at last and Leigh seemed
about to follow her. A weak sigh of relief escaped
Jassy's lips. A few more minutes and she would
be able to get away. She had to go, even though
that crazy masochistic streak in her longed to stay,
simply to be in the same room as the man she
loved so desperately.

Lost in her thoughts, Jassy was unaware that
the crowd around her had thinned as people
headed for the supper table, and she was now
clearly visible from the door. As Leigh turned he
glanced around the room, nodding an abstracted
greeting to several people he knew, and too late
Jassy realised the vulnerability of her position.
Before she had time to move those tawny eyes
were on her, narrowing swiftly in shock, and
Jassy's stomach clenched in panic as she saw that

shock fade to be replaced by a coldly burning fury.

The room seemed to whirl around her, the noise of the party fading to a dull murmur, the faces of the other guests blurring before her eyes while Leigh held her transfixed with that steely golden gaze like a small, terrified rabbit held paralysed by the hypnotic stare of some predatory hunting cat. In spite of the fact that only seconds before she had felt unbearably hot, Jassy's blood had now turned icy cold, so that she felt she would never be warm again.

Then Leigh moved, taking a single step towards her, and abruptly the spell was broken. Turning swiftly, Jassy blundered blindly through the crush of people, heedless of murmurs of protest. She was conscious of nothing beyond the need to put as much distance as possible between herself and Leigh, so that when she reached the patio doors the led out into the garden she didn't hesitate, but fumbled with the catch, breathing a silent prayer of thanks when she found it was not locked. A few seconds later she was outside, taking deep, gulping breaths of the chilly night air in an effort to calm her racing pulse.

Only then did she realise her mistake. The garden was really only a small, square courtyard, enclosed on three sides by a high wall, the fourth side of the square being the house itself. The only way out of it was to go back through the patio doors, back into the brightly lit room where even now Leigh was hunting her like some jungle tiger balked of its prey.

At that moment a slight movement caught Jassy's eyes and she turned towards the house again, freezing in shock as someone stepped out into the garden, the light from the room behind him catching on the brightness of his hair.

'Leigh!' The word was just a whisper, barely stirring the night air as Jassy glanced desperately round for some way of escape. But there was nowhere she could go; she was caught like an animal in a trap. Panic-stricken, she moved even closer to the wall, praying that its shadows would hide her.

The noise she made was very slight, almost imperceptible, but Leigh heard it and his head swung round swiftly, his eyes narrowed against the gloom. He spotted Jassy almost at once, and headed straight towards her, keeping his eyes fixed on her pale face all the time. Without a care for the damage she might be doing to her clothes, Jassy edged nervously away, her back against the wall.

Leigh caught up with her just as she reached the farthest corner. He arrested her attempt at flight by the simple expedient of placing one hand on either side of her shoulders, his long fingers resting on the brickwork, his body directly in front of her, blocking out the light from the house so that he was nothing but a black, threatening shadow that towered over her menacingly. His face was in total darkness, so that Jassy could not make out his features, but the rigidity of his stance told her that his expression would be as hard and unyielding as the rough stones that were digging painfully into her back.

'So this is where you've been hiding.'

Leigh's voice was quiet, but with a cold, cutting edge to it that made Jassy feel sick with dread. She knew this mood and feared it, recognising the signs of that almost unnatural control that was far more dangerous than if he had actually raged at her.

'Well, now,' Leigh continued goadingly, 'and what is the beautiful Miss Richardson doing here, I wonder? Hoping to give the casting couch another try, are you, my sweet?' His tone turned the endearment into an obscenity. 'Don't you ever learn? It didn't work out too well the last time, did it?'

Anger at the injustice of his suspicions drove away Jassy's fear.

'Even *your* mind can't be as warped as that!' She flung the words at Leigh's shadowed face, attacking blindly without a thought for the possible consequences. 'You know perfectly well that Benjy used to be my tutor—you can't possibly imagine that I might be trying anything with him! And for your information, Benjy's wife happens to be a very good friend of mine and I don't go around breaking up my friends' marriages—so don't judge everyone by your own standards, Mr Superstud Benedict!'

The silence that greeted her outburst terrified her, making her wish her rash words back. But it was too late and they seemed to hang on the cold night air, forming an intangible yet powerful barrier between them. Leigh's eyes gleamed dangerously in the moonlight, his very stillness infinitely menacing.

'What a shrewish tongue you have in that pretty head of yours,' Leigh said at last, and the black cynicism of his tone came as almost a relief to Jassy, who had expected a more violent reaction. Her chin lifted as she faced him defiantly.

'What did you expect? Did you think that I was going to let you slander me again and accept it meekly without hitting back? Well, you'd better think again. I have as much right to be here as you have—as Benjy's *friend*, nothing more.'

Leigh's momentary hesitation told her that he had caught that important 'again' and it had made him stop to think. He straightened up slowly, taking his hands from the wall and pushing them deep into the pockets of his trousers, watching her closely all the time. His movement meant that the light from the house fell fully on Jassy's face for the first time, and as it did so she heard Leigh draw in his breath sharply. She couldn't understand why that faint sound should make her feel afraid, but it did. It was not the fear of Leigh's ability to hurt her emotionally that she had felt from the moment she had first seen him, nor was it the purely physical terror she had experienced only moments before, but somehow it combined the two and yet was subtly different from either one.

'I think I'd better go in,' she said hurriedly, her voice shaking with nerves. 'Benjy will be wondering where I've got to. He——'

'No!' Leigh's voice was harsh. His hand caught her arm as she tried to move past him, swinging her round roughly.

'Let me go!' Jassy's high, fear-filled voice sounded sharply in the silence of the night.

'Not yet,' Leigh growled. 'I have things I want to say to you.'

'Well, I have nothing to say to you—and I doubt if you could possibly say anything I would want to hear! I'm going inside. It's late and I'm c-cold.'

Jassy's voice shook noticeably on the last two words. Leigh's hand on her arm seemed to burn through her blouse, scorching the skin beneath the silky material, and in spite of her fear she could feel the familiar, intoxicating sensations creeping through her, warming the blood in her veins so that she was intensely grateful for the darkness that hid the colour in her cheeks. It was hopeless! Leigh had only to touch her like this, even in anger, his grip hard and cruel, and she was lost, ready to fall into his arms without a thought for her own safety.

'Here.'

To her astonishment, Leigh was pulling off his jacket, releasing her arm only for a second as he did so. He draped it over Jassy's shoulders, pulling the lapels closely round her neck. Jassy felt the sensual touch of the velvet, still warm from the heat of Leigh's body, smelt the painfully evocative scent of his aftershave that clung to the soft material, and closed her eyes against the pain of the memories that assailed her.

'Now,' Leigh said softly, his hands still on the lapels of his jacket, effortlessly holding her prisoner, 'I think I'm going to kiss you.'

Jassy's eyes flew open in shock, her face drained of all colour in the moonlight.

'Don't you dare! I mean—Leigh—no!'

She struggled impotently against his restraining hands, twisting her head desperately from side to side, but Leigh simply took one hand from his jacket and caught hold of her chin, turning her face irresistibly towards his. Jassy had one terrifying glimpse of the wild, malevolent glitter in his eyes before the blond head bent and his lips captured hers.

For one stunned second Jassy froze in shock, for Leigh's kiss was not the fierce assault she had anticipated, but soft and sensually teasing, evoking a response deep inside her. Then, drawing on the few shattered remnants that were all that was left of her ability to think clearly, she put out her hands to push Leigh away from her, only to find to her horror that they refused to obey her. The fingers she had intended to flatten against his chest to force him from her curled wantonly around the buttons on Leigh's shirt, tugging at them impatiently until they yielded, and she slid her hands inside the soft silk. She heard Leigh's ragged sigh before his mouth hardened on hers, his kiss no longer gentle but filled with a fierce, demanding passion that forced her lips apart, taking everything she had to give.

The garden, the darkness, the party in the house behind her all faded from Jassy's mind.

Even the paving-stones beneath her feet seemed unreal and insubstantial. The one thing that existed was Leigh, his arms now around her in a grip so powerful that she feared he would crush her completely. After the long, lonely weeks of wanting, longing, dreaming of just such a moment as this, and knowing her dreams to be hopeless, she was overwhelmed by the intensity of her response. She was swept along on a tidal wave of passion, returning Leigh's kisses with an eagerness she did not attempt to conceal, her body arched towards his, pliant against his hardness.

Leigh's hands were moving softly but insistently over her, his fingers closing possessively over the soft swell of her breasts under the white blouse, driving her to a fever-pitch of excitement where there was no room for self-consciousness or shame. She was beyond thought, heedless of the fact that Leigh's jacket had slipped to the ground, conscious only of the wonderful things his lips and hands were doing to her. She was clinging blindly to him, murmuring her need of him in soft, incoherent words when he pulled himself away from her abruptly, removing her clutching hands and holding them in both his own, his body held stiffly away from her. His breathing was slightly uneven, but apart from that he showed no sign of the passion that had been such a tangible force in him only seconds before, and his sudden cold detachment turned Jassy's heated blood to ice.

'Now we're even,' he ground out harshly. 'Now you know what it's like to want someone so much you're aching for them—only to have them freeze you out at the last minute. It isn't pleasant, is it? I should know—I've been there.'

Fear, shock, and bitter frustration deprived Jassy of the ability to speak. She could only stare at Leigh in anguished disbelief, a phrase she had heard him say—a lifetime ago it seemed—repeating over and over in her head. 'I reckon I owe you one, and I don't forget easily.'

'Now perhaps you'll be a little less eager to try your seductive little wiles on some other poor fool.' Leigh's taunting words lashed Jassy like the sting of a whip as he let her hands drop suddenly and began to fasten his shirt with fingers that were only very faintly unsteady.

'You're detestable!' Jassy choked on the words. 'I wish I'd never met you!'

'The feeling's mutual.'

Leigh's sardonic retort was the last straw. 'Oh, why don't you go to hell?' Jassy exploded, driven to the limit of her self-control.

Inexplicably, shockingly, Leigh's mood changed suddenly, the savage, tormenting look fading swiftly from his face.

'I did once,' he said bleakly. 'I reckon I'm still there.'

Jassy's confusion was total, the world tilting crazily around her so that she reeled sickeningly, reaching automatically for Leigh's arm for support. He made no move to help or repulse her, but simply let her hand rest on his arm, regarding her silently with dark, unfathomable eyes. Very slowly the world righted itself again and Jassy swallowed with difficulty, wetting her lips nervously before she could speak.

'I—I don't understand.'

'Don't you?' Leigh questioned harshly, but the fierce, attacking quality had gone from his voice. He shrugged dismissively. 'Why should you understand? I don't even understand myself. What is it about you, Jassy?' he went on with soft intensity. 'Why is it that even now I can't stay away from you? It's like a sickness. I know what you are—a cheap little tramp who'll sell her body to anyone if that's the price of stardom, but when I knew you were here I had to come looking for you. I couldn't settle till I found you. I told you once I was half demented with wanting you; now I think I'm completely, incurably insane.'

The beautiful voice was thick with self-disgust and Leigh shook his head slowly as if in despair at his own foolishness.

'So now you know,' he finished, his tone bitterly derisory. 'I hope you're satisfied.'

Roughly he shook off the hand that still rested on his arm, then bent and snatched his jacket from the ground, slinging it over his shoulder before striding away towards the house without another word. Jassy watched him go, too bewildered by his abrupt change of mood even to try to understand what he had meant by his enigmatic words, until the cold began to impinge on the trance that held her captive and she shivered convulsively. Without Leigh, the garden seemed very dark and threatening, so she followed him hurriedly, suddenly afraid to be alone with her thoughts.

Benjy accosted Jassy as soon as she re-entered the room.

'There you are! I've been looking for you everywhere. I promised you were going to meet someone special, and now I'm going to deliver. This lady is the one who tried to help you before. Yes, I know it didn't work out, but she took a great interest in you from the moment I mentioned your name—because, of course, she'd seen you as Juliet.'

And then, of course, Jassy knew exactly who he meant. She moved as if sleep-walking, every step seeming to be performed in slow motion, one face standing out from the crowd around her, a cold, proud face, crowned with a coil of red hair.

'Anna, darling, I want you to meet a friend of mine. This is Jassy Richardson—my Juliet.'

In the stillness of that moment Jassy sensed someone standing silently at her back and a cold, shivering sensation running down her spine told her exactly who it was without turning to look. Anna did not seem to have noticed Leigh's silent presence, but to Jassy the atmosphere seemed to crackle with a tension that was almost tangible as Benjy continued blithely.

'Jassy, it was Anna who arranged the audition for *Valley of Destiny* at such short notice.' He announced the fact triumphantly, like a gambler producing his trump card, then stared in bewilderment as a nerve-racking silence greeted his words.

'Anna!'

It was Leigh's voice that shattered the silence, and in the second before she spun round Jassy saw how the actress's face paled underneath her make-up, making her look, not like the regal movie queen she had always appeared to be before, but a lost and lonely woman, so that instinctively Jassy felt a pang of sympathy for her. But from the moment she saw Leigh's face all thought of anyone else was driven from her mind. His expression was dark as a storm-cloud, the tawny eyes mere slits in a face that was white with fury. Every muscle in his body was rigid with a tension that communicated itself to the people around him, silencing their animated chatter. Jassy thought that she had seen Leigh angry before, but never, ever like this.

'Is this true?' Leigh demanded ominously.

The few seconds' pause before he had spoken had given Anna time to regain some degree of composure.

'I did it for you, Leigh,' she said, her voice high and sharp. 'It was obvious that she wasn't just the secretary she claimed to be, but one of those little leeches you've always had such trouble with, so I arranged the audition so that you could see just what a scheming little bitch she is!'

'No!' Jassy tried to protest, but Leigh's eyes were fixed on Anna.

'There's more to it than that,' he declared inimically. 'I want the whole truth, Anna.'

Jassy was shaking uncontrollably, this sudden turn of events sending her into a state of shock so that she was only dimly aware of Benjy's arm coming around her protectively.

'Honeybun,' he said quietly, 'I've got the most dreadful feeling I've boobed again. This looks suspiciously like the start of World War Three, and if I know Anna things are going to get very nasty indeed. Let me take you out of here.'

Unresistingly, Jassy let him draw her away towards the door. Neither Leigh nor Anna saw her go, and the image she carried with her as she followed Benjy was of the two of them standing tall and proud in the middle of the room, their eyes locked together and the sparks of anger, like flashes of lightning, almost visible between them.

CHAPTER TEN

Jassy knew she should go to bed. It was almost three in the morning and she was achingly weary, every muscle in her body crying out in protest at being deprived of rest, but she knew that sleep would be impossible when her mind was so agonisingly wide awake.

She had promised Benjy that she would go straight to bed when he had left her at her flat over an hour before, but knowing that she should sleep and being able to do so were two completely different things. She couldn't sleep without knowing what had happened between Leigh and Anna after she had left the party.

Benjy had taken her downstairs to the warm, friendly basement kitchen, and had pressed a drink into her trembling hands.

'You wait here while I go and do my duty as host. I'll have to try and persuade those two crazy people to do their fighting somewhere else. Please don't look so devastated, honeybun. Anyone who knows Leigh has seen this coming a mile off. He's been making it plain that he's sick of Anna's clinging, and I reckon tonight just about finished it. I should have known better than to invite them both on the same night,' he added wryly.

Alone in the kitchen, Jassy had waited tensely, straining her ears for some clue as to what was going on upstairs. Twice she heard the slam of a door and the roar of a car's engine, but that was all, and when Benjy returned he gave her only the briefest outline of events. Anna had stormed out and Leigh had followed her, driving after her 'like a bat out of hell,' Benjy said appreciatively, seeming to have enjoyed the whole experience. Then he had insisted on driving Jassy home.

'It's the least I can do, honeybun. I never meant to get you entangled in Leigh and Anna's private civil war. And I promise, after this, no more good turns. They don't seem to turn out quite as I plan them.'

Now, sitting in the silent flat, Jassy wished she could break down and weep to ease the aching tension in her heart, but her eyes were painfully dry, burning with the tears she couldn't shed as she forced herself to review her relationship with Leigh though her heart cried out against such self-imposed torture. But she couldn't hide from the truth any more. She had condemned and rejected the women who had seen only the golden public image Leigh projected, but in her hurt pride at his non-appearance at the performance of *Romeo and Juliet* she had made assumptions, blind, foolish assumptions of selfishness and arrogance that had stayed with her, preventing her from really getting to know the man behind the persona of the Golden Thief. Now it was too late. She had seen tonight that the barriers Leigh built around himself, barriers that had started to come down when he was with her, were back in place and stronger than ever.

A sudden sharp knock at the door brought Jassy's head swinging round to stare in the direction of the sound as if she could see through the thick wood. When the knock was repeated, she froze, panic-stricken, her breathing swift and shallow. Who would call at her flat at this time?

'Jassy, I know you're in there, I saw the light.' Leigh's voice coming clearly through the closed door did nothing to soothe Jassy's fear. Irrationally, she felt she might almost have preferred some manic prowler. 'Jassy! Open this door!'

'Go—go away, Leigh!' Jassy forced the words from a throat that was unnaturally tight with tension.

'Not until I've talked to you,' was Leigh's implacable response. 'If you don't open this door I swear I'll break it down—and I don't give a damn who hears me.'

Jassy's apprehensive glance went towards the room in which Sarah lay sleeping. She could have no doubt that Leigh fully intended to carry out his threat, and if he did her friend would be sure to waken.

'All right—just a minute,' she said hastily, hurrying to turn the key, then stumbled back as the door burst open and Leigh strode into the room.

He looked totally dishevelled, the grey velvet jacket discarded somewhere, his face drawn into lines of strain, and his golden hair falling in disorder across his forehead. Seeing him, Jassy's heart twisted and she longed to smooth the tension from his face with gentle hands, but she knew that the time for such displays of tenderness was long gone. Leigh would only interpret any gesture of love as another attempt to seduce him and would repulse her attentions violently.

'What are you doing here, Leigh?' she asked, the tension that gripped her making her voice hard. 'In case you haven't realised, it's nearly three in the morning.'

'I know.' Leigh's voice was strangely quiet, the grim, threatening note gone from it completely. 'I would have been here earlier, but I had to check that you weren't still at Benjy's first—and I had to go home to get this.'

He pulled a thick envelope from his pocket and held it out to Jassy, who stared at it blankly, not moving to take it.

'Take it!' Leigh insisted. 'I brought it for you.'

'What is it?' Jassy asked hesitantly.

Leigh's mouth twisted wryly at the suspicion in her tone.

'The terms of surrender,' he said cryptically. 'Or, to put it another way—a contract.'

Jassy's heart gave a painful lurch and she found that she couldn't breathe properly. None of this could really be happening!

'I—don't understand——' she began, but Leigh broke in on her.

'I'm giving you what you wanted,' he declared harshly. 'The part of Clara—it's yours—that contract says so.'

The pain was white-hot; Jassy couldn't believe that anything could hurt so much.

'I don't want it, Leigh,' she said flatly.

'But you have to take it! It's all I have to give you. It's your part—it always has been. I knew that as soon as I saw you that night outside the drama college, when the film was still only an idea. You were in my mind when I wrote it—why the hell do you think I came to see you in *Moonrise*? It certainly wasn't to see the bloody play!'

Jassy's head was reeling. She had forgotten that Leigh had told her that he had seen her act in that ill-fated production, had forgotten his enigmatic comment that 'the *play* was appalling'.

'I knew then you were my Clara, that no one else would ever do. I've been comparing every actress I've auditioned with you and no one even comes close. If you don't take the part, no one else ever will. I'll scrap the film, forget the whole damn thing.'

The tears that had refused to fall earlier were there now, stinging Jassy's eyes. Leigh was offering her the part she had dreamed of, but the dream had turned into an appalling nightmare. She could never accept it, not like this, because to do so would only reinforce his belief that the part was all she had ever wanted, that she had used him for her own selfish reasons. In despair, Jassy turned away from Leigh, bending her head to hide her tears.

'Don't do that!' Leigh groaned. 'Jassy, don't turn away from me! I know you must hate me,

and I don't blame you—I've treated you appallingly. But please let me do something. If you'd
prefer it I won't even direct the film—I'll hand
it over to someone else. Jassy, please! I know you
don't want my love, but at least let me give you
this.'

Jassy's eyes were wide open, but she could see
nothing. Time seemed to stop, the moment
hanging suspended, as she took in what Leigh had
said, then, very, very slowly, she came back to
reality. Behind her she heard Leigh's despondent
sigh as he flung the contract on to the table and
she swung round hastily to see him moving towards the door, his head down.

'Wait a minute,' she said, and at first thought
he hadn't heard her because shock had weakened
her voice. Then he turned back and the empty,
defeated expression in his eyes tore at her heart.
There was no sign now of the Golden Thief, just
a man—the man she loved.

'You'll take the part?' Leigh asked, his voice
dead, no hope, nothing in the dull tones.

Jassy's smile was very gentle as she shook her
head.

'No, Leigh,' she said quietly, 'I'll not take *that*.'

She emphasised the last word clearly and,
bruised as he was, Leigh noticed and frowned his
bewilderment.

'Then what...?' he asked slowly, and Jassy's
smile widened.

'What else were you offering?' she teased
softly.

Leigh's hands went to his temples, pressing hard against them as if to ease some intolerable ache, his eyes closed.

'I didn't——' he began, then his eyes flew open and Jassy saw a faint spark in their tawny depths. 'You don't mean—you can't—Jassy, the only other thing I mentioned was love!'

The raw emotion in his tone caught at Jassy's heart, so that her own voice was infinitely tender when she answered him.

'I know,' she said clearly. 'And that's the only thing I want from you.'

There was a long, tense pause, then, 'Forgive me if I've got this wrong,' Leigh said stumblingly, 'but are you saying you *love* me?'

'Oh, Leigh,' Jassy sighed. 'Did you really not know? Yes, I love you—I love you with all my heart.'

The stunned expression still hadn't left Leigh's face. 'I don't see how you can,' he said dazedly, 'not after the way I've treated you, the things I've said. Oh, Jassy, I never meant to hurt you! I loved you so much—I think I fell for you the moment I saw you. You looked like a small, angry kitten spitting at me and I was lost.' A slightly crooked smile curved Leigh's mouth. 'I couldn't keep my hands off you, but you made it very clear that wasn't what you wanted.'

'I didn't know what I wanted,' Jassy put in quickly. 'I'd never felt like that before and I was scared.'

'I know.'

Leigh's tone was very serious. He had taken a step back towards her—just one, but it was a start.

'That Friday night, when I calmed down, I realised that, but then I really thought I'd blown it completely, especially when you were so unflatteringly honest about your opinion of me, and I decided I'd better forget the whole thing. But then on Saturday, when I was at Anna's, all I could talk about was you. I couldn't get you out of my mind, and in the morning I had to see you—I couldn't wait till you got to the office—so I called to offer you a lift. I'd planned to be oh, so polite, to take things very slowly, but you wouldn't let me. First there seemed to be another man with you, and I found I was as jealous as hell, then you fought me every step of the way until I couldn't think straight. The only thing I knew was that I wanted you, so I told you so—hardly the most subtle approach! I know I blew my top over the script, but by the time Steve got to me I'd already had to admit to myself that it wasn't the *script* that was important, and that wasn't something I was exactly prepared for because up until then my work had been my life.'

Leigh paused, frowning slightly as if still reeling from the impact of that realisation, and Jassy waited silently, knowing intuitively that he needed to tell things in his own way.

'I didn't know it then, but that change had been creeping up on me for a while—ever since a small blonde spitfire had let rip at me a couple of years ago.'

The lop-sided smile returned as Leigh caught Jassy's swiftly indrawn breath.

'My mother's experiences—the mess she'd made of her life—had made me wary of any emotional relationships, and I determined that that wasn't going to happen to me. My work I could handle—it was under my control and so I put everything I had into it. Success was the only thing that mattered.'

'I know how that feels,' Jassy murmured. Hadn't she done exactly the same thing in her own way, letting her life be ruled by her determination to prove herself to her parents, not letting other sides of herself, particularly her emotional side, develop?

'Perhaps that's why you got to me so strongly. I must have recognised the same sort of obsession in you, and suddenly everything looked so very different. I thought I had everything I wanted, but somehow it no longer seemed enough—it was a damned empty way to live. I was restless, there was a huge gap in my life, but I couldn't put my finger on where it was. I thought *Valley of Destiny* would fill it—I thought it *had*, because when I came back from Scotland and started work on it again I found a new meaning in everything I did. Then it hit me that it wasn't the film that was doing this to me, but you.'

Leigh's hand reached out to Jassy, his gesture tentative, hesitant, and, sensing his need, she took several hasty steps towards him and clasped it firmly. Leigh's fingers curled around hers tightly as he went on.

'In the middle of that week I was supposed to be at some high-flying dinner party, but I just couldn't face it. The only person I wanted to be with was you—so I found myself here, sitting on that appallingly uncomfortable settee, drinking very flat cider and loving every minute of it. I'd spent all afternoon putting on the public face for that reporter, but with you I could relax—I didn't have to play a part any more.'

That was the night he should have been at Anna's, Jassy recalled, and shivered as she remembered the actress's words. 'If you're wise, you'll get out now, before you regret it for the rest of your life.' At the time she had thought that Anna was simply referring to her belief that Leigh could never love anyone, but, hearing those words in her mind in the light of tonight's events, she saw them for what they really were—a threat that Anna had carried out to devastating effect.

'But you were so different from the other women I knew, and I didn't know how to handle them.' Leigh seemed not to have noticed Jassy's momentary abstraction. 'Looking back, I think I avoided anyone who might threaten the way I thought I wanted to live my life, so I knew only the Gemma Morgans of the world, which reinforced my prejudiced view of the female sex. And I was so used to holding back, not letting people see too much, that I didn't know how to tell you what I was feeling. And I was impatient; I wanted to grab you, hold you any way I could. Suddenly the film didn't matter, success didn't matter, without you, it was all empty—nothing. Then, just when I thought that maybe you felt something too, you turned up at that bloody audition and I went completely crazy, thinking you'd just used me. I wanted to lash out, destroy everything that was important to me—and I damn nearly succeeded!'

Leigh turned to Jassy, his eyes very dark and intense.

'You couldn't have loved me then.'

'But I did,' Jassy assured him confidently. 'I never stopped loving you.'

'You mean, even in the middle of that whole bloody mess... Hell, I could kill Anna!'

The ferocity of Leigh's expression frightened Jassy, but it was not that that made her heart lurch painfully. She had known that, inevitably, they must come to Anna Golden, but now the time had come and she was not sure she was quite ready.

'Jassy,' Leigh said quietly, 'about Anna...'

Jassy wanted to stop him, tell him that Anna was in the past, that she didn't matter, but she knew from his face that he wouldn't accept that and, deep down, neither could she. Anna had tried to come between them, and in a way she was still there, an invisible, vindictive presence that had to be exorcised so that there would be no doubts, no questions left unanswered.

'Tell me about Anna,' she said simply.

Leigh sighed tiredly, raking his hands through his already ruffled hair.

'Anna's a very lonely woman. Underneath all that sex goddess act, she's a rather inadequate human being. She's had three husbands and none of them stayed around for more than a year, her career's a mess, she's terrified of growing old, losing her looks, being alone. I cared enough for her in the past to want to help her.'

'You're not her lover,' Jassy said, making a statement, not asking a question, but still she saw Leigh's golden head move in angry denial.

'I was once—years ago, for a very short time. It was dead before it ever hit the papers, and there had been nothing between us before she and Carrington had officially separated.'

'But he cited you——' Jassy was interrupted by Leigh's groan of self-disgust.

'I know—dear lord, I know! That was one of the biggest mistakes of my life. Look, Anna and I had a very brief affair, one that burned itself out before it had really begun—but Anna wanted a quick divorce from Carrington, so she gave him my name as her lover. I'll admit I went along with it, on the advice of my agent—the worst advice I've ever been given in my life. If I'd known what it would lead to——'

Leigh broke off, shaking his head at his own foolishness.

'Jassy, I was just twenty-two, and my career was beginning to take off. The Anna Golden affair helped my image.' Leigh's tone was wry. 'I was my agent's despair, I was being billed as the new sex symbol, but there wasn't a woman in my life—and that can start some very nasty rumours. So I let myself be seen with Anna, let the papers think there was more to it than there was just for the publicity. I was pretty bloody naïve because I never expected it to snowball as it did.' A twisted smile flickered across his mouth. 'Needless to say, I have changed agents since those days.'

'But that Sunday—when you came to my flat——' Jassy made herself say it.

'I'd been at Anna's all night?' There was a flash of the old fire in Leigh's eyes. 'Dammit, Jassy, I'm quite capable of staying the night in a friend's home without dragging her into to bed with me! And that's all Anna is—was—a friend. Oh, I know she tries to make it out to be more than that, her career's on the skids and mine is riding high, so she uses me for publicity as I once used that damned Golden Thief nickname. I put up with her play-acting because it didn't touch me— except in one way. Whenever I look at Anna I see my mother—she was about Anna's age when she died. I couldn't help her, but if being seen with me stops Anna from going the same way then it's the least I can do. My friends all knew the truth, so it didn't matter—until now.'

The muscles in Leigh's jaw tightened, drawing his mouth into a thin, hard line.

'She's never done anything like this before. I suppose she must have realised from the way I talked that you were a real threat to her position in my life. When you told me she'd come to the office that day I knew I'd have to have it out with her, tell her things couldn't go on as they had been, but I had to get those damned auditions out of the way first. Then, when we were at the theatre, I got a phone call from Benjy——'

Leigh broke off abruptly, his eyes shadowed with remembered pain so that Jassy's heart twisted inside her at the thought of how he must have felt. He had to make an obvious effort to speak again.

'But after tonight I doubt if Anna will ever want to see me again. It's just as well I was desperate to get back to you because when I found out how she'd arranged the audition to make it appear as if you were only using me I was strongly tempted to break her selfish little neck! Loving you the way I do, and thinking I'd lost you because of Anna, I felt positively murderous!'

Leigh's hands clenched convulsively at the memory, then a moment later he opened them suddenly, lifting them in a gesture that dismissed Anna from his thoughts, and, remembering the glimpse she had had of the sad, pathetic woman behind Anna's careful façade, Jassy knew that she could understand why he had tolerated her for so long, but that now she too could dismiss her from their lives.

'I do love you,' Leigh said, his eyes very dark and sincere. 'You do believe that, don't you?'

Jassy could only nod, too full of happiness to speak as Leigh drew her gently towards him.

'I have something very important to say,' he murmured, causing Jassy to glance up at him in some confusion. What could possibly be more important than hearing Leigh say he loved her?

'Marry me, Jassy,' Leigh said simply. 'Marry me and take the part of Clara. If we're together it can't fail—but I can't do it without you. I need you with me, at my side wherever I am, whatever I'm doing. Of course, if you really don't want the part, I won't force it on you. You can do anything you want if you'll only say you'll marry me and let me love you as I've wanted to from the moment I saw you.'

The tiger's eyes were intent as Leigh lifted Jassy's face towards his. He must have read her answer in her own eyes, but Jassy still had to speak because there was one thing she had to make very clear.

'On one condition,' she said quietly, refusing to let the uncertain, questioning look in his eyes distract her as she went on determinedly. 'I must have another audition for the role of Clara—and you mustn't have anything to do with it. Steve knows what you want—let him decide. I want that part desperately, but only if I'm good enough, not because you want to give it to me. All I want from you is that man you offered me. I want you for yourself, not because of who you are.'

The silence that followed her words left Jassy in no doubt that Leigh had understood the importance of what she had said. He drew a long, ragged breath, and when he spoke his voice was distinctly unsteady.

'That's a condition I have no intention of arguing with. On those terms, then, what's your answer?'

'Yes,' Jassy told him unhesitatingly. 'Yes to marriage, yes to Clara, but above all, yes to having you love me—I wouldn't want any of the others without that.'

'There's no chance of that,' Leigh declared huskily. 'I'll have myself written into your contract just to make sure.'

At last every trace of doubt and uncertainty was wiped from his face, and there was no holding back now as he pulled Jassy close up against him, his arms fastening tightly around her waist. His kiss was long, deeply passionate and completely perfect—perfect because it was the first kiss they had shared safe in the mutual certainty of each other's love. Jassy didn't know if it was minutes or hours later that Leigh lifted his head with a reluctant sigh, cradling her against his side, her cheek resting on the warm strength of his chest, his hand stroking her hair with infinite gentleness.

'I think I'd better let you get some sleep,' he said unwillingly. 'Though it hurts like hell to leave you.'

Jassy's smile came easily. Confident in his love, she gave him a soft, enticing look.

'Then don't,' she whispered cajolingly. 'Don't leave me—take me with you.'

'Don't tempt me.' Leigh's voice was a husky mutter. 'Right now, I can think of nothing I want more—but I forced the pace last time, rushed you into things though I'd said I could wait. This time will be different.'

'But you only said you'd wait until I could tell you I wanted you,' Jassy challenged lovingly, moving very slightly away from him in order to see him more clearly.

She searched his face, looking deep into his eyes, finding in them a flame of love and longing to match the one that burned in her own heart.

'I'm saying it now, Leigh, the waiting's over. Take me with you because I want you, my love—I want you more than I can say.'

Later, Jassy was to reflect that she should have known. It was inevitable that, having got their hands on a good catchphrase, the papers would be reluctant to let it go, even when it was clearly obsolete. On the morning after their wedding every popular newspaper carried a photograph of Leigh and Jassy together, their happiness clear for all the world to see, and above it ran the caption: 'The Girl Who Stole the Heart of the Golden Thief.'

Take 4 bestselling love stories FREE

Plus get a FREE surprise gift!